WHERE THERE'S A WILL

BY
LUCINDA JANE PERRY

Thanks for dedicating
a few precious hours of
life to reading my simple
story. Your friendship &
support has enriched
the hours of my
own life —
Cindy

INKWATER PRESS

PORTLAND • OREGON

Cover and interior designed by Masha Shubin

www.inkwaterpress.com

ISBN 1-59299-053-3

Publisher: Inkwater Press

Printed in the U.S.A.

ACKNOWLEDGMENTS

To my husband, Dean, not only for supporting my schemes and dreams, but providing the means by which I might achieve them. He claims to be my biggest fan. I hope he knows I am his.

To my sister, Sara, for her contributions toward the imaginative concept upon which this book is based.

To Jan, my editor, writing coach, friend and occasional therapist, for her strong encouragement and gentle guidance. Without her this book may never have come to fruition.

Author's Note:

This book is a work of fiction. Any direct correlation to actual persons, places or events is unintentional on the part of the author. However, if any disreputable characters described in this book reminds you of someone in your own family, you have the heartfelt sympathies of the author.

PART ONE

THE FUNERAL

CHAPTER ONE

Hattiesville, Arkansas, population 473. A small but long-standing community built on a foundation of farming, raising hogs, and of course, family. Or, as in our case, family feuding. Inside the funeral home the air was sticky with humidity and rain threatened outside. Having easily predicted the weather would be just so from years of traveling to that burg, I had defiantly, yet discretely, protested the wearing of pantyhose underneath my long skirt. Such conduct from me would surely have been considered trashy had anyone noticed, particularly my Aunt Oretta, who liked to put a scandalous spin on even my most inconsequential behaviors, and possibly by my own mother, Estelle. I looked down at the pantsuit my sister, Carolyn, was wearing and suspected she was a partner in crime, wearing knee-hi's at best. Of course, it wasn't anything to remark on if she was wearing what those older women considered to be less than proper attire because she had two children and was hoping for one more with what was now her fourth husband. A much better track record according to our family than my being divorced once and not having remarried. Especially since I had no children. My mother and aunt just could not understand me. I am, after all, supposed to be the beauty in our family, which isn't saying much, just that I am somewhat slender and can make a fair showing on a good hair and make-up day. But to them, women were put on this earth to marry and raise children. Period. The fact that I had earned a Master's Degree, been professionally employed for years, owned my own home and car, had made wonderful long-term friends, and traveled to some interesting and even exotic locations over the years was unremarkable to those two women. I mean, gee, I hadn't even had the decency to get knocked up. In or out of wedlock. Loser.

As predictable as the weather was the surety that some form of pork would be served before the funeral service. In fact, now that I am almost forty, I can sum up the summers spent on my grandparents' Arkansas farm in two words: mud and ham. I strongly dislike both. It appears, however, that blood is thicker than mud, too, because I found myself in Hattiesville once again. My sister, Carolyn, and I had packed up our mother and hauled ourselves clean across the state of Kansas and the better part of Arkansas to gather with family. My mother's family, that is, the Clankton clan. And believe me, clan is the appropriate term. As in the Hatfield clan. Or the McCoy clan, depending on who's side of the feuding you were on. Like those infamous families, the Clanktons, too, were in a constant state of battle over past resentments and current arguments. The occasion that had brought us all together again was my Grandmother Iola's funeral. My mother's mother.

In the chapel of the funeral home, Carolyn and I were seated in the second row with the other grandchildren, all of us using our programs as fans in the stifling heat and humidity. The director of the funeral home had told us the air conditioning unit had been turned on but it would take a little while for it to kick in and cool things off. He explained it was usually not so warm and muggy that time of year and they had not yet utilized the unit that season. Right. I, for one, was not familiar with any time of the year when Hattiesville was cool, dry and breezy. It was either warm and muggy or cold and clammy. Either way, your hair would be limp and your clothes stuck to your skin by 10:00 a.m.

While we cousins had been settling ourselves in, our parents, the four Clankton siblings, had assembled themselves in the front row just ahead of us, from left to right: Aunt June, Uncle Nedd and his wife, Donna, our mother, Estelle, and Aunt Oretta with her husband, Lou. Now, all of the members of the Clankton clan knew the politics behind that particular seating arrangement. It was far from random and was most important in keeping the peace, even during that solemn occasion.

Yes, the seating arrangement alone told quite a story in itself. For example, anyone in the Clankton family could have told you that Aunt June was on the very end as she was only on speaking terms with Uncle Nedd and his wife. And Aunt June was probably the most "normal" of the entire lot. The others all went downhill from there, in my opinion. Anyway, June and her sister, Oretta, had been in a state of non-communication for years over an argument about selling their mother's, my grandma's, farm land. June claimed Grandma wanted to sell the land once she went into the nursing home as she would not be going back to the old farmstead. June thought it would be a good idea to sell the land and invest the money for Grandma. Now, it came as no surprise to the rest of us that Oretta would balk at that idea. You see, Grandma's land butts right up against Oretta's land and her husband, Lou, and son, Jason, had profited from farming that ground for many years. They also leased some land from Grandma for which they received payments from the government to leave "unfarmed." Why those federal land payments just didn't go directly to Grandma, I didn't know. Grandma could have left that land "unfarmed" as easily as the next person. Surely Oretta and her husband weren't paying more money to lease the land from Grandma than they were receiving from the government. It had always seemed fishy to me but, hey, I was just one of the kids. However, it didn't sit too well with the rest of the Clankton siblings, either, as it appeared that in "managing" Grandma's land, Oretta and Lou had assumed all profits, as well. Grandma's land had been a hotly controversial topic among the Clankton siblings for years.

Anyway, I didn't know the exact details of that particular clash, but Aunt June accused Aunt Oretta of breaking into her briefcase during the night and going through her private papers, destroying the real estate contract that Grandma had signed for June. June was to turn those papers in to the land agent the next day. After a heated confrontation in Oretta's living room, June packed up her bags, determined never to return to Oretta's home or speak to her again. To date, she had held true to that declaration. And, as a result, my Aunt Oretta and her family continued to "oversee" Grandma's land for the remaining years of her life.

Sitting next to my mother, Estelle, was also ruled out for Aunt June as their last encounter ended with Aunt June forcing Mom out of the car, luggage and all, onto the lawn of the city of Jonesboro, Arkansas's police department. Now, to an outsider that may sound like harsh treatment of a seventy-five-year-old woman recovering from her second battle with cancer. Unless, of course, you've ridden in a car with Estelle for any extended period of time. That is to say, it was not the first time Estelle had been left off unceremoniously by the side of the road when the driver of the vehicle could tolerate no more of her verbal abuse and hostile behavior. My father, for one, fell into that category and I must confess that I, too, had been pushed to the point of pulling off on the shoulder of the highway in more recent years. Once, when I was getting ready to enter high school and not yet old enough to drive myself, I had my mother pull over to the shoulder so I could get out of the car and walk home. A body can only take so much and Estelle just will not let up.

Things being as they were, then, I didn't hold the Jonesboro incident against Aunt June. After all, that type of thing had gone on between the Clankton siblings for decades. I just knew from the start it was a bad idea for Mom and Aunt June to drive to their high school reunion together. Two Clanktons in the cramped confines of a car for any extended period of time can only lead to trouble. But those two were determined.

Aunt June had come to Colorado for Mother's first breast cancer surgery just the year before and they had been getting along splendidly over the phone ever since. I guess they were feeling giddy with sisterly love when they decided to venture onto the open road together. Unfortunately, and as predicted, being in close quarters for a day or two was enough to start their Clankton blood boiling.

It all worked out okay in the end, though. It seemed the Jonesboro police force was very understanding and helpful, though I am sure they were quite puzzled by the circumstances that brought my mother to their door. And, oh yes, you can be sure my mother, Estelle, told them every intimate detail of the sordid event. The version where she was innocent of all blame, of course. Taking pity upon my elderly mother (as those who don't know her often do) and not knowing what else to do with her, some kind officer drove her to the local bus station and helped her acquire a bus ticket to get to St. Louis. From there she purchased a plane ticket and flew back home to Colorado. Needless to say, Estelle and June hadn't spoken to each other since that day, but that had not kept Mom from speaking about her sister. Mom had spent countless hours trashing Aunt June on the phone to Uncle Nedd and Aunt Oretta and to anyone else who would listen to her. So, it came as no surprise to anyone at the funeral to see Aunt June seated on the end by her brother, avoiding her two sisters at all costs.

At the moment, Uncle Nedd was on speaking terms with everyone, although it had only been a year or so since my mother, Estelle, had thrown a glass of water on him at the breakfast table during a visit to her home in Colorado. I had just entered the kitchen that morning while my uncle was sopping his face with a napkin. Having been Estelle's daughter for almost forty years and, therefore, having long been numbed to that sort of hostile behavior, I simply poured myself a glass of juice and asked Uncle Nedd, "Was it about Dad?" He just nodded and said, "Yep." Nedd had clearly mentioned my father in some way, a taboo even some twenty years after my parents' divorce, and had received the natural consequences of such. Uncle Nedd was usually a bit quicker to forgive and forget a spat and he did not take the incident too seriously or too personally. As a result, Uncle Nedd and Mother had been on fairly friendly terms recently, calling periodically and sending a note now and then.

As for Aunt Oretta, she was currently on good terms with Nedd and Estelle, but not with June, as you will recall. Now that didn't mean Aunt Oretta had been on good behavior particularly. A sore note with all three of her siblings for years had been the fact that Oretta had never visited the homes of any of them. Not in her entire life. Ever. And Nedd lived only about two hours away! I was convinced that my Aunt Oretta could not make herself visit her siblings as it would mean having to acknowledge that something of theirs might be superior to something of hers. Which just about all of it would be, unfortunately. I guess her take on it was that what she didn't know wouldn't hurt her nearly as much as having to pay a compliment to one of her siblings would. But, since all of her siblings were there in Hattiesville on her turf, as usual, Oretta seemed to be amiable enough to the two (Nedd and Estelle) and was just ignoring the one (June).

As a side note, I should mention where the mother of those four contentious children, Iola, my grandmother, had historically fit into the scheme of things. Except for her physical and mental deterioration those past few years, Grandma Iola had always been right on the front lines of battle. In fact, there were few things she relished more in her life than the high emotions of a rousing Clankton family scrap. It sure got her blood circulating. There was little doubt in anyone's mind then, that on that day, Grandma would normally have been strategically seated somewhere among her four children in the first pew, were her place not predetermined to be up at the very front of the chapel, as is customary at one's own funeral.

So, as things stood, from the behavior of the Clankton siblings throughout the visitation period and by their choice of seating order, it was clear that the circumstance of attending their mother's funeral had not altered the current camps of war. And, war was exactly how I had come to think of that family and its ongoing commitment to jealousy, greed, competition, hostility, and even downright violence. The feuding began way before I came onto the scene if you believed the stories told by my brother who is fifteen years older than me. Oh, yes, the battle was ongoing, but the camps of war did change periodically, usually as a result of some sort of despicable behavior from one of the siblings, leading to a catastrophic upheaval of current allies. And it was exactly that which concerned me most at that moment, for despite the cloying heat and humidity in the funeral home, my blood had suddenly run cold, sending a shiver of anxiety down my spine. I sensed the winds of change in the air and was certain that the camps of war were about to shift yet again.

The cause of my inner turmoil came just as the organ music began to play, signaling everyone to take their seats as the memorial service was about to begin. My sister, Carolyn, and I had just seated our mother, Estelle, in the front row and slipped into our own seats behind her when Aunt Oretta made one of her claw-like grabs at my arm and hastily whispered into my ear, "After we leave the cemetery, Libby, we all need to go directly to the lawyer's office for the reading of Mother's will."

I cannot tell you how completely stunned I was, which was probably a good thing because the service was getting underway and I wouldn't have had a chance to comment anyway. Boy, Oretta had good timing on that one, the old viper. Actually, she struck so quickly it took me a few minutes to realize what was so disturbingly wrong about that bit of information. After all, it was a funeral and the reading of wills and settling of personal belongings and estates was sure to follow. Nothing unusual there, really. Oh, really? Hmmm. On second thought, it seemed rather inappropriate and downright tacky to go to the lawyers office right from the burial service. It sort of felt like brushing the dirt off our hands so we could grab a copy of the will. Couldn't the meeting with the lawyer be done the next day even? Everyone who didn't already live in that mud hole was staying another night anyway. Shouldn't we spend the time visiting (those who were speaking to each other), reminiscing with colorful stories of Grandma over the years, etc.? But no, it seemed that in true Clankton fashion, Grandma's life was going to be reduced to what was really most important to her children: what she had and who gets it now that she's gone.

That very subject was the second factor contributing to my intestinal distress. Grandma's will had always been a much discussed and passionately argued issue, speculated upon by all four Clankton siblings. However, Iola's husband, my grandfather, Robert, died some 20 years earlier and left a very clear and fairly divided will at the time of his passing. In reading that document one got the feeling that Grandfather knew his wife and squabbling offspring very well and did his best to leave things in a responsible manner; taking care of his wife and providing for his children equally after her death. The question that remained was whether Grandma had left things alone, or had Grandfather's good work been tampered with? If the will had been altered, it would not have been done without assistance from one of her children, as Grandma had led the simple life of a somewhat backwards country woman. Having only an eighth grade education and marrying my grandfather at the ripe old age of 15, she was pretty content to let her husband take care of such matters. After all, he was an older man and an educated school teacher to boot. Besides, Grandma deeply revered Grandfather, especially after his death, and would never have changed anything he had done on her own. Furthermore, neither would, nor could, Grandma have taken it solely upon herself to make an appointment with a lawyer and discuss the legalities of altering the will her husband had so carefully laid out.

Yep, if there was going to be anything new to report on the settling of my grandmother's estate, you could be sure one of the Clankton siblings had a heavy hand in it. Making the appointment, driving Grandma to the lawyer's office, interpreting and advising all along the way. Yes, indeed, if Grandma had changed her will as many times as she had changed camps in the Clankton family war over the past years, siding with a different child each time, the whole thing was sure to be a mess and anyone's guess as to who was to profit and who would be excluded.

As if the timing of the reading of the will and the possible contents of the very will itself weren't enough to evoke a wary caution in me, there was yet a third factor that was weighing heavily on my mind. The very fact that we were told about the will reading at the absolute last minute before the service started, leaving no time to discuss or react, stunk to high heaven. Not only had we all spent the entire morning together, eating at the church (requisite ham), and greeting guests attending the service there at the funeral home for the past two hours, but we had all arrived two days earlier! That's right, it was two days previous to the funeral that Carolyn, Estelle and I had arrived at Uncle Nedd's house in St. Louis. Oh, we went to dinner, visited all evening and even spent the night there before heading down to Arkansas. It was not a surprise drop-in either as we had planned our trip with everyone days in advance. The next day we had driven Mom down to Hattiesville to her sister Oretta's home, also. Visiting my Aunt Oretta was something I personally dreaded and usually wormed my way out of but, considering the occasion that time, I bit the bullet and went along. We spent the day at Oretta's farm, ate a light supper with her family (ham again), and then headed off to the hotel rooms we had reserved in town. Now, during all of that time spent together discussing the funeral, all of that family togetherness, not one person so much as hinted about the reading of the will. No discussion about when it should be read, that an appointment had been made, nothing. Not one word. Something was definitely brewing on the day of the funeral and I suspected it wasn't anything good.

Since it had been Oretta who had dropped the bomb on me at the last possible moment, she was immediately placed on the list of probable culprits in devising any unsavory scheme regarding Grandma's will. Her timing was too well-planned for her to simply be passing the information on after receiving it herself from one of the others. No surprise, really, as that was quite her style. Oretta was known for her subterfuge and quiet deceitfulness and I was certainly feeling as if we had been deceived for two whole days. The only remaining question was did Uncle Nedd and/or Aunt June have prior knowledge of the appointment with the lawyer? My best guess was Aunt Oretta had either worked alone (with her husband, Lou) in manufacturing some kind of hostile takeover of Grandma's will, or she could possibly have been in cahoots with her brother, my Uncle Nedd. Since she and Aunt June hadn't been speaking, at least to my knowledge, it was unlikely June was in the know unless Nedd had included her in some "side deal" of sorts. I believed the guilty parties, perpetrators of yet another possible wrongdoing against their siblings, were the ones with knowledge of the appointment with the lawyer well in advance of that eleventh hour. As soon as the service was over, I intended to do a little detective work to find out who knew what, when.

In the meantime, I sat in that chapel in dreaded silence, contemplating the meaning of the news I had just received. The most I could do at that moment was to scribble a brief note on the program I held informing my sister, Carolyn, of the upcoming events of the day. After reading my message, I could tell that Carolyn's brain was undergoing a similar process of deduction, for we each seemed to be in a thoughtful state of reverie, broken only by an occasional moment of eye contact and a knowing look. But, in those brief moments, I could see in her face what must be reflected on my own; fear, dreaded trouble, dirty business.

CHAPTER TWO

Finally, the memorial service was about to wrap up. I was feeling some guilt about having spent the bulk of that time trying to figure out who the players were behind the arrangements for the deceptively innocent will reading, rather than reflecting on the loss of my grandmother. I took comfort in knowing, however, that Grandma herself would have been far more interested in a brewing family feud than in the formalities of having herself laid to rest. One could even get an eerie feeling that under such circumstances, Grandma was gleefully smiling down on us all from heaven, if heaven was indeed her destination. My attention was brought back to the events at hand at one point during the service, as I was surprised to discover it was Uncle Nedd's children who had gone all out by making themselves available to "perform" at Grandma's memorial service.

For the most part, I had always liked all of my cousins in the Clankton clan, particularly Uncle Nedd's twins, Jimmy and Johnny. I didn't know if the knot in my stomach about the pending visit to the lawyer's office was making me suspicious of everyone, but nothing seemed to be settling well with me about that whole day by then, not even what should have been considered touching and sentimental under such circumstances. It may have been true that I was assigning ulterior motives to everyone's behavior, trusting no one, questioning everything, but I use the word "perform" to describe the contributions made that day as they just seemed to smack of insincerity. For example, Jimmy and Johnny gave an oration they had composed together - a personal and often humorous ode to our grandmother. It was well written and did capture much of her character, I admit. However, it was most definitely "performed" between the two of them, an act they had worked out in advance complete with facial expressions, timely pauses and the playing off of each other's leads. That wasn't too surprising, really, if you knew that both men had dedicated their lives not so much to their actual teaching professions at the high school level, but to being the advisors of the speech, debate and drama clubs there that were their true passions. Since the spotlight generally went to their students in those organizations, perhaps the funeral service was an opportunity for them to impress that small town crowd with their talents on stage. The temptation of a captive audience had proved too strong for them to ignore, it seemed.

I would vouch that was most certainly true of the performance of Tamera, Uncle Nedd's stepdaughter, who sang one of Grandma's favorite hymns during the service. Sweet, I know. But, I was also aware of the fact that Tamera hardly knew Grandma as Nedd's wife, Donna, and her children were fairly new to the Clankton family fold. It was no secret, either, that although Tamera did not sing professionally she would desperately like to be doing so. And believe me, that gal could create a captive audience, if necessary, by backing people into a corner to listen to her. During the past few years of our acquaintance I had been trapped into more than one of Tamera's vocal performances in Uncle Nedd's living room. A funeral home packed full of folks holding a program with her name in it was certain to be enormously appealing to Tamera, regardless who was being buried.

Now, no doubt such a showing from his own children filled Uncle Nedd not only with pride, but with a fulfilling sense of one-upmanship towards his sisters. Ah yes, his children were showing love and support for the family through that most difficult time. Malarky! I had long ago learned to be suspicious of most things where my mother and her siblings were concerned and even those supposedly meaningful, soulful tributes from my cousins were not above question!

For one thing, I found it odd that none of Aunt Oretta's five children had made contributions to the service, even though they had grown up right next door to Grandma and Grandpa all their lives! In fact, they were the only ones who lived in Hattiesville at all over the past several decades. My cousin, Jason, farmed their land even at that time. Neither he nor any of his four sisters had anything to share about growing up next door to Grandma? Strange, too, that no one had asked Carolyn or me if we wanted to contribute in any way. During all of that planning and putting together of a memorial show, er, I mean service, no one mentioned to us that any of the grandchildren were standing up, nor did they seek our interest in doing so. I am not saying either of us would have spoken, necessarily, but it seemed a bit odd not to at least have been asked since they knew we would certainly be attending Grandma's funeral. Maybe it's just that reciting, singing or reading poetry didn't readily spring to mind for Carolyn and me as we lacked that showbiz mentality. It appeared auditions were held privately at Uncle Nedd's house well in advance, giving the performers ample time to practice and prepare.

As for Aunt June's two boys, Mark and Carl, they didn't even show up for their grandmother's funeral. Long ago, they decided to remove themselves from the outrageous group of people into which they were unfortunate enough to have been born. Smart move. Heck, even my brother, Reese, fell into that category. It was no surprise to anyone that Reese did not show up for that occasion or any other. He had long held the belief that the Clankton siblings were a pack of hyenas who would sell each other, their mother, and possibly even a child or two of their own for personal gain of some sort, especially financial. He has said our own relatives were some of the most lying, cheating, self-serving people he ever had the misfortune to know. Family or not, my brother Reese had neither cared about nor communicated with a single Clankton family member in over thirty years, with the exception of Estelle, our mother. Sometimes even that proved more than he was willing to tolerate and it was not unusual then, when he did visit, if his date of departure from her house occurred a bit sooner than originally planned.

As the organ music once again played, finally signaling the end of the service, Carolyn and I stood up and looked at each other with raised eyebrows as if to say, "Let the battle commence!" While Carolyn moved forward to help Mother out to the car where it was lined up with the others for the procession that would take us to the cemetery, I sidled up to Aunt June as she, too, was heading for the door. It was time for my detective work to kick in. Very calmly and casually, acting as if I were just verifying the day's agenda, I asked, "So, are we going to the lawyer's office directly from the cemetery?" June said, "Yes, I guess so, Libby. I was just told about all of this when I sat down next to Jim at the start of the service."

Now, I deduced from her somewhat flustered demeanor that Aunt June was also quite taken aback at the hastiness of events, as well as having been informed at the last possible minute. There was no doubt she, too, was agitated about what might possibly await us all after Grandma's burial. Clearly, Aunt June had no prior knowledge of events and I therefore deduced she was an innocent party in that surprise attack. I quickly informed her that we, too, had found out about the reading of the will ourselves from Oretta, just as the service was starting. Aunt June raised an eyebrow and nodded silently as she took in that news. Taking a deep breath, she declared that she was not one bit surprised. And, having said that, Aunt June squared her shoulders, lifted her chin and set her face for battle, then headed out the door.

Well, now I was down to Uncle Nedd. Had he received the news from Aunt Oretta just before the service and passed the information on to Aunt June at that point? Or, was he, like Oretta, behind some covert operation regarding the will and had known what was going to take place all along? Was there a scheme so well planned out that Nedd and Oretta had chosen a conquer and divide strategy, where she was to take charge of Estelle, and he June? Just how deep did the deception go? Hmmm, again.

As one might imagine, the trip from the funeral parlor to the cemetery was a very short one in that small town and we did not even get the air conditioning in the car cooled off enough to relieve us before we arrived next to my grandfather's grave. As a pallbearer, Uncle Nedd had ridden at the head of the procession in a limousine and was preoccupied with his assigned duties, but I saw his wife, Donna, walking with her songbird daughter, Tamera, across the grass to the grave site. Using the same, already once successful strategy of playing innocent, I caught up to them, walked along side of Donna, and asked if we were going directly from there to the lawyer's office. Donna responded, very specifically I might add, that the appointment was at two o'clock and if we were early we could get a cool drink at the cafe while we waited. Whoa! That sounded to me like someone who not only had prior knowledge of the details but had even thought out the time frame of our agenda. It didn't look good, but it looked pretty clear.

As the crowd gathered around the grave site I moved in closer to Carolyn and Mom. Once again, my sister and I were not in a position to speak openly and I could only give her a 'we need to talk' look. Clearly, we were going to have to find an excuse to separate ourselves from the crowd and from our mother, Estelle, as soon as the service was over. We couldn't talk in the car as we had not yet told Mom that her mother's will was being read that very afternoon. We were unsure what Mom's reaction would be. In her prime, the nastiness from Estelle, the oldest sibling, would have already been in full swing, funeral or not. She might have started a shouting match in the parking lot of the funeral home or even on the cemetery lawn, for that matter. Whatever form our mother's outrage might have taken, I guarantee it would have been one ugly scene.

Although Mom could still get worked up pretty darn good, she was in a rather diminished state of health at the time of her mother's funeral. By then, she was recovering from her third bout with cancer, couldn't hear beans, glaucoma had reduced her vision somewhat and, let's face it, her mental health had always been rather questionable. There had been no improvements on that front, either. When we had first arrived for Grandma's funeral two days earlier, I could tell that my cousins were taken aback that their spitfire of an aunt seemed quite frail. As a result of her current physical and mental status, Carolyn and I were unsure if news of the will reading would send Mother into a rage or if she would even understand what was happening and why it was cause for concern. Either way, we felt the need to protect her, and ourselves a bit, and to first get a full understanding of what the hidden agenda behind the hurried reading of Grandma's will was really all about.

As the few roses and first sprinkles of dirt were placed over Grandma's casket I was, for the first time that day, overcome with sadness. Could it be true, I thought, that even on the day of her burial, Iola's children, the contemptible Clankton siblings, were about to be embroiled in yet another battle of selfishness and greed? Unbelievable. "Now be honest," I told myself, "It is not only believable, it is very likely to be true." Oh, heck, of course it was true.

Finally finding our moment to converse privately during the departing of guests, with a heavy heart, I informed Carolyn of what I had learned and what I feared. Namely, that Aunt June seemed to have been caught by surprise with the news of the intent to read Grandma's will on the same day of her funeral, as we had, and that Aunt Oretta and Uncle Nedd together appeared to be behind those arrangements. Also, because we were now running out of time, we needed to tell Mom about the appointment with the lawyer. We couldn't risk sitting her down in that legal office without at least giving her an idea of the reason she was there.

The other thing I had begun to realize was that one of us, either Carolyn or I, would have to sit in on that meeting with our mother for the reading of the will as she was unlikely to hear, let alone understand, what was being said by the lawyer. We certainly couldn't trust the information second-hand from any of the other Clankton siblings, even Aunt June, because if there had been foul play where Grandma's will was concerned, June was sure to be hopping mad and likely to distort things in her anger. The question was, who would go? Actually, there was no real question about that. I knew my sister too well. I would have to go. I didn't want to, but I knew that I would be the one. And I was right. Carolyn immediately stated she wanted to avoid that scene entirely because, even though she was certainly interested in what was going to take place in that office, she also knew it was going to be a stressful and possibly hostile scene and she was likely to get upset herself and spout off. She wanted me to go in and get the information as I was more likely to remain calm and objective. Have you ever noticed how people always compliment you when they want you to do something they wish to avoid? That decision having been made, all we had left to do was to inform our mother of the meeting and head to the local cafe to wait out the appointed gathering time with Hattiesville's only lawyer, a Mr. Lawrence P. Baylor.

The cafe, also the only one in town, was a rundown, dirty little place with no charm that a glance around the room could discern. Although I was a bit hungry after foregoing the ham before the funeral service, I opted only for a cold drink, hoping it would come in a bottle, gambling on a clean glass if not. Conversation among our group was rather stilted; polite chit chat from most, a forced casualness from Uncle Nedd, I felt (or at least imagined). Aunt Oretta seemed to be doing her best to present a facade of disinterest in the upcoming meeting. Aunt June was sullenly quiet and Estelle, our mother, was prattling on about the funeral service, the nice weather and how pleased Grandma would have been with the turnout that day.

For once, amazingly, our mother was actually the most appropriate in her demeanor and comments. That was due, of course, to the fact that she had no real idea of what was about to take place. In the car, on the way to the cafe, Carolyn and I had told her we were to meet with the lawyer that afternoon to discuss Grandma's will, but Mother had shown little concern and, thus, was completely unaware of the tension in the room. Poor Mom. She was not in a state of mind or health to jump into things with both barrels blasting as she would have normally been inclined to do. If Mother were in better form the battle would have been in full swing by that point. No way would we all have been calmly sitting in that cafe sipping iced tea and soda.

As the clock approached two p.m., I announced to our little group that I would be attending the meeting with my mom and would be happy to drive everyone over to the lawyer's office in Carolyn's spacious van. That caused a bit of uncomfortable hemming and hawing, gathering of handbags and pushing back of chairs. Oretta quickly rallied, however, and said she wanted to drive over so she could give her sister, Estelle, a ride in her new Lincoln and declared that Mother and I would ride with her. Now, June would walk over, and it was only about two blocks away, before she would get into a car with Oretta. Not that June was invited to ride along in the first place. Conveniently, and with perfect timing, Nedd piped up and said he and June would drive together and meet us over there. It seemed like a lot of commotion over such a short drive. That uneasy feeling crept back into my bones as I noted that the end result of that little tussle put the two people who seemed to be "in the know" literally in the driver's seat, while the remaining two sisters were divided and driven over separately. Divide and conquer again?

Mr. Lawrence P. Baylor's office was right across the street from the county courthouse (where else?) in a low slung white clapboard building. Mr. Baylor himself was standing at the door in anticipation of our arrival. He was a rather tall figure in a dark suit, boasting a full head of wavy white hair and the unmistakably bulbous red nose of the lifelong alcoholic. He approached Oretta in a grinning and jovial manner as we were getting out of her vehicle. He admired her new Lincoln and asked if that was the same one she had taken him out for a spin in last week. Oops! Cat's out of the bag! It seemed my aunt had paid a visit to that lawyer just the week before and had been on chummy enough terms to take him for a drive around the block in her new car. Lordy, Oretta was guilty as sin. She knew it, too, by the way she made an attempt to glide right over his little remark with quick introductions of Mother and me. Better yet, she knew I knew, as I could not resist giving her a quick smirk and a raised eyebrow to let her know just how interesting I found that lawyer's innocent slip of the tongue. I doubted that Lawrence P. Baylor had caught his own error for, although he was not outright drunk, he had clearly lubricated his system prior to that gathering. Who could blame him really? After all, he was one of the few with full knowledge of what was in my Grandmother Iola's will and he had known the Clankton clan for decades. I imagined he could pretty closely guess what trouble would follow when those two entities clashed.

As we all entered Mr. Baylor's modest office, I looked around, wondering where he discreetly kept his hooch. That whole scene was like something out of another place and time for me. Was I really sitting in that close little office, sticky with humidity, waiting for a small town lawyer who was a bit snookered to read Grandma's will to the four cutthroat Clankton siblings? It was the event dreaded for years by all of the spouses and children of those four siblings and it was hard for me to digest that I was in a situation to have to witness the sordid affair firsthand. Mr. Baylor had not expected me to be included in the party, either, and he had to bring in another chair from the outer room that served as his reception area. I had little concern the chair would be missed out there; it would be an unusual day indeed in a town that small for two parties to seek the council of a lawyer at the same time. What were the odds?

All right. The final moment had arrived. There was no more cause for delay. The tension in that room was much too thick for small talk and certainly no pleasantries were going to be exchanged. Grandma's will now had to be read.

June and Nedd were sitting on a small sofa, while Oretta sat ramrod straight in a hardbacked chair next to Nedd's side of the sofa. Mom and I were across from them in two chairs placed in front of Mr. Baylor's desk. My aunts and uncle were all sitting very still. Aunt June bore a tight-lipped expression, intent on hearing every word and its nuance. Uncle Nedd appeared somewhat relaxed but was also looking at the lawyer, anxious for him to speak. Aunt Oretta sat with her hands in her lap, no noticeable expression on her face, except for the gleam in her eyes.

As for me, I was poised with pen and notepad in hand, while Mother nonchalantly picked lint off her skirt and examined her fingernail polish. When we had told Mother of the reading of the will she had been very unconcerned about it, believing that her father had divided everything equally and they already knew about his will. She felt the meeting that day was only a necessary formality and she simply trusted I would take care of the details that involved her. She truly suspected no ill-doing from any of her siblings. Her reaction showed us just how out of touch she was getting in those days. Gosh, Carolyn and I knew how limited Mother was at that time and were STILL afraid to tell her about the reading of the will after the funeral. We figured it could be the one thing that would break through the fog that enveloped her and she might rally for the showdown. And, hey, having lived around Estelle for any period of time, one learned to act with caution at all times. It was a hard habit to break and we just didn't want to risk getting caught off guard. As it turned out, we need not have worried. Mother was oblivious to any possible wrongdoing by her siblings and was, therefore, quite amiable. She was the only one in that room doing any talking and was sharing her opinions on several completely irrelevant topics. Lord, help me, I silently prayed.

The next moment, in a moderate voice, well-practiced and with a barely detectable slur from his liquid courage, Mr. Baylor gave us all a quick greeting and a brief introduction. He was wasting no time and seemed intent on settling Iola Clankton's estate as soon as possible. He started, actually, with the will my grandfather had so carefully laid out years before, pointing out that everything was indeed left to my grandmother, Iola, and that at the event of her death, all land, capital and other assets shall be divided equally among the four siblings. I actually took a deep breath in relief, thinking my overactive brain had gotten me all worked up over nothing. It was going to be okay. Things were just as my grandfather had left them; fair and equal. I smiled toward my aunts and uncle, casting my suspicions aside and eager to be back on friendly terms with them all. I was ready to head back to the cafe, apologize to Carolyn for getting both of us all worked up over nothing and spend the rest of the day visiting with the Clankton family.

But then, that lawyer brought out a codicil to Grandfather's will my grandma had worked up there in that very office under Lawrence P. Baylor himself over fourteen years ago. I had breathed too soon. At least one of the four Clankton siblings had been up to no good and I had a pretty good idea of who. Aunt June was apparently on the same mental track as I was as she asked outright if Iola had come in by herself at that time or had she been with another individual? Mr. Baylor covered well, stating that he held to the auspices of confidentiality and could probably not recall the specifics of an appointment from almost fifteen years ago anyway. Although I was inclined to believe the latter part of that statement as he couldn't remember the exact color or make of the car he had ridden in just last week with Aunt Oretta, I felt Mr. Baylor knew exactly what had happened back then and how it was going to play out at the time of Iola's death. And, unfortunately, that day had come.

Yep, as it turned out, I should have stuck with my original conviction that something was awry. The contents of the codicil Grandma had legalized confirmed my every suspicion of those last few hours. Grandma had signed the statement with her own hand, yes, but with someone else's hand on her elbow, no doubt. The codicil stated Grandma had left one thousand dollars each to June and Estelle and divided the remaining money equally between Oretta and Nedd. Now, we were not talking about a vast fortune there necessarily - maybe one hundred thousand dollars or so in all. Not that the amount mattered. It could have been ten thousand dollars or one thousand dollars and, for those four siblings, it would still have been worth cutting each other out, screwing each other over and getting in a final blow. So, roughly speaking, Nedd and Oretta would receive about fifty thousand dollars each, while June and Estelle received the bequeathed one thousand dollars - just enough to keep them from being able to contest the will. After all, they had not been written out completely.

Now, the reaction of the Clankton clan to that news was most interesting to me. Aunt Oretta said virtually nothing, making eye contact with no one she was related to, looking only at Mr. Baylor as if awaiting further information. Oh, so innocent. Aunt June, on the other hand was hot, shaking her head and saying she had known Oretta would do something dirty like that. Uncle Nedd took on the role of peacemaker by saying that it would all be okay. "We'll make it right, don't worry about it now," he soothed. As for my mother, Estelle, she hadn't heard a word that had been said but seemed to take comfort in her brother's willingness to take care of whatever problem her sister June was in a snit about. As far as Mother was concerned, she was ready to get out of there. I informed Mom there was more to hear yet from Mr. Baylor and I would explain it all later. Content with that explanation, she turned her attention back to cleaning her glasses and commenting on the humidity level in the room, which I thought may be rising due to the steam spouting from Aunt June's ears.

Once we had all settled back in again, Mr. Baylor continued by covering what was to happen with Grandma's farm land. It seemed that there, Grandfather's original will had not been tampered with. The farm land was to be sold and the money divided equally among the four Clankton children. Well, I thought, that was at least one decent thing in the whole situation.

Having reviewed the entire contents of the will, the meeting ended rather abruptly. Aunt June was up and out of that office with Uncle Nedd following close behind, encouraging her to get into his car so he could drive her back to the cafe where her own vehicle and husband awaited. She really had no choice and, since Nedd still seemed concerned about "doing right" by everyone, she opted for a ride with him. Mother, still without a clue as to what just occurred, willingly got into Oretta's car, making remarks about June's rudely executed departure from the office. Not having much choice myself, since Mother was already sitting in the car, I got into Oretta's new Lincoln, too, and from the back seat attempted to get her to break her silence by drilling a hard stare directly into the rearview mirror as we also made our way back to the cafe. Alas, Oretta chose not to make eye contact with me, nor did she utter one single word, despite what had just taken place in that lawyer's office. In fact, once we arrived at the cafe she did not attempt to get out of her car or even turn off the engine. Gee, I don't think she even bothered to shift the gear into the park position. Oretta simply pulled up next to the joint and let us out in the gravel parking lot. She did lean over from the driver's seat and say, "Bye, Estelle. Bye, Libby," just before I shut the car door behind my mother.

Now if that wasn't a classic Clankton clan farewell on the day of their mother's funeral, I didn't know what was! Wasn't it just the day before that Oretta had us in her home, fed us all (ham, remember?) and acted as if everything was right as rain? After all, Oretta and Estelle were in the same war camp! Or so we thought. Regardless, even now, it was clear to all that Mother didn't really know what had taken place in that meeting. She was sickly, feeble, and unable to comprehend much of what was happening around her. Ironically, perhaps of them all, Mom was truly there for her own mother's funeral and held no other agenda. Granted, that was not necessarily by choice but simply as a result of her own compromised well-being. Anyway, that one act, of dropping Mother off in the parking lot with no more than a wave of the hand, was the final seal on my opinion of Aunt Oretta. Although all of the siblings were of questionable character, Mother included, I had always held a special dislike for Oretta... and she for me. On that day she had proven the depths of just how low she was capable of descending. Didn't she know her triumphant takeover of Grandma's money, her smug good-bye and curt wave of the hand were lost on her sister, Estelle? Who could wallow in that kind of ill-gotten glory? Maybe those gestures were meant for me, who was fully aware of just what had taken place that day. Perhaps that was enough for Oretta.

Once inside the cafe, I found the news had been shared with the others who had waited there during our brief absence. June was making her disgust with the situation widely known but seemed to be laying the blame entirely on Oretta while exonerating her brother, Nedd. That was no doubt due to Nedd's continuing concern to right any wrongs. He seemed to be intent on calming everyone's nerves and assured us all that it would turn out all right. Despite being somewhat sedated by Nedd's soothing words, June's parting remark was that she would be contacting her own lawyer to review the legalities of her mother's codicil to her father's will, and to ensure that the land was properly assessed and sold at a fair market price. She said she wasn't going to let Oretta end up getting that land for a song by pulling another fast one. And, I must say, future events later proved that June had called that one pretty close to home.

Left now in that grimy local eatery were Uncle Nedd and his wife, Carolyn, Mother and me. Awkwardly, our travel plans at that point included staying that last night with Nedd and Donna at their home in St. Louis. I didn't feel good about it and could see that Carolyn was uneasy, too. For one thing, we were eager to find a private place and time to fully discuss all that had taken place on that auspicious day. Mom, on the other hand, was ready to move on to St. Louis and meet up with Nedd's children for a nice dinner out somewhere. It was becoming harder already to watch Mother unknowingly carry on in good spirits toward Nedd and Oretta, when all evidence pointed to wrongful behavior on their part against June and her. I wanted to believe Uncle Nedd had the best interest of his sisters at heart - but I also knew it wasn't likely, as it would be the first time he placed concern for his siblings over that of himself. Altruism was most certainly not a Clankton family characteristic - especially if that person stood to lose anything in the process.

I guessed at some point Carolyn and I would have to decide whether or not to clue Mom in on what was really going on currently among the fearsome Clankton four. On the one hand, she had a right to know, as it really involved her directly, and my sister and I were just the messengers at that point. At the same time, it was a shame to have to inform Mom that her own mother had written her out of any cash inheritance. And, to learn that news on the day of her funeral just seemed too much to burden her with at the moment. Mother was, after all, the only one spending the day reminiscing on times spent with Grandma and Grandpa. The rest of us, me included, were shamefully embroiled in the newest Clankton family battle. My vote was to let our mother grieve in peace. Besides, I needed some time to process that mess and think about the best way to handle things.

CHAPTER THREE

For the time being, there seemed no other recourse but to keep our mother, Estelle, comfortably shrouded in ignorance and to go through with our original plans for the evening ahead in a polite and civilized fashion. We all met up at a Chinese restaurant once we arrived in St. Louis, and Nedd's children, our cousins, were informed of the details of the will as Carolyn, Mom and I sauntered our way through the buffet. Now, normally I am all for a buffet of any kind as I love to dabble in little bits of all kinds of different foods but I was feeling too heavy of heart to enjoy that night. That was partly due to the fact as I sat down with my food my cousin's wife offered her condolences to me by saying, "Oh, Libby, we're all so sorry about what your grandmother did to Estelle." I wanted to tell that woman just how clueless she was, how little she knew about anything that went on that day. I wanted to tell her that the person who very well may have done wrong by Estelle was wolfing down a crab wonton across the table from us at that very moment. I wanted to scream. What I did was give a tight smile while biting my tongue and nodded my head briefly. Needless to say, it was a strained meal and I was tiring of polite banter. It seemed to have been a day full of such trivialities, masking my true suspicions and emotions, trying to remain neutral in the face of yet another dastardly deed within the Clankton family, and never finding time to vent privately with Carolyn. My sister was the only person with whom I was desperate to engage in some real heart-to-heart conversation and the only person I dared trust by that time.

As we prepared to leave the restaurant the drizzle that had lingered in the air all evening finally cut loose and turned itself into an official downpour. We had endured scores of similarly drenching outbursts in that part of the country but that particular one seemed to further dampen my spirits. I just wanted to get away from those people and get all the way back home to Colorado as soon as possible. I had to settle, however, for the bit of solace to be found on the third floor of Uncle Nedd's expansive home in an affluent suburb of St. Louis proper.

Staying on the third floor at Uncle Nedd's home was the equivalent of staying in a three star hotel. There were three bedrooms on that floor, each with their own private full bathrooms. All of the rooms were beautifully decorated with coordinating wallpaper, linens and towels, and a cable TV was tastefully displayed in each room for overnight guests as well. Once there, Carolyn and I went to our separate rooms, peeled out of our funeral garb and donned some cool shorts and tops, then met in my room where we were finally able to discuss the events of the day on a full scale.

Carolyn was more distressed about what had happened that day than I had realized. I should have guessed that would be so, really, as she can get pretty worked up about things herself. And, Carolyn is very passionate in her beliefs about what is right and what is wrong. The trouble with that is sometimes hers is a blind and unbending righteousness that doesn't always consider the gray areas. She is quick to rush to judgment, forgiveness is rarely an option and her view of the matter is the only accurate perspective. With Carolyn, things are pretty black and white, all or nothing. It can irritate the heck out of a person.

I tend to be just the opposite. I will play with an issue for way too long, trying to determine what else could be behind the situation. Giving people the shadow of a doubt, even when things are pretty clearly laid out, is my annoying specialty. I want to consider the place the other person is in and what the feelings are that might be motivating their behavior. I will question my own feelings to try and determine what is really bothering me about whatever has happened. I want to give people a chance to do the right thing. Talk to them. See what I mean? I can weary a situation to death. I tend to swim around in the gray areas until I drown the subject altogether. I, too, can irritate the heck out of a person.

Although we certainly tended to handle things differently, Carolyn and I were both pretty shocked by what had happened that day and were quite disgusted by the Clankton siblings' behavior once again. That any one of them could take Grandma's codicil to Grandpa's will seriously was, to us, a complete farce. After all, the writing of that codicil took place some fourteen years ago and only served to indicate who was in cahoots in the ongoing Clankton war on that particular day. The camps had fluctuated numerous times over the years since then. To Carolyn and me it was unthinkable that any of those four outrageous people would attempt to rationalize that they were somehow more deserving of Grandma's money than the rest of their own sordid lot.

After kicking around our disbelief at the turn that trip had taken, Carolyn and I did decide two things that night at Uncle Nedd's house: 1) we would not tell Mom how Grandma had cut her out of the will, but we would inform her that the land was to be sold and the money from the sale divided equally, and, 2) I would go downstairs and feel Uncle Nedd out about his stated intentions of "putting things to right," as he had been exclaiming all afternoon and evening. I, of course, felt that if I could sit down and talk with him it may clear up a few things and hopefully ease our troubled minds. I had always liked Uncle Nedd and wanted to give him the benefit of a doubt. Carolyn had always liked Nedd, too, and wanted to tar and feather him. There was that difference between us again.

I found Uncle Nedd downstairs sitting by himself at the kitchen table, almost as if he was expecting me. I asked him if it was okay to talk for a little while about what had happened at the lawyer's office earlier that day. He said sure, let's discuss it. Nedd seemed rather relieved to hear that Carolyn and I had decided, at least for the time being, to keep Mom in the dark about the negative aspects of Grandma's will. He assured me that it was the best thing to do.

" I agree with you girls, Libby. There's no need to burden your mother with all this business about the will," he said. "It would only hurt her." Well, his answer was no surprise to me as that certainly made things easier for him. He avoided the wrath of his sister, Estelle, and continued to look like a good guy. But, hey, the jury was still out on Uncle Nedd and I was there to give him a chance at redemption.

I wanted to approach Nedd in a way that made it seem we were obviously on the same side of the issue, as I was still hoping we might actually be. So, I agreed with what he had said and added that it would indeed be unnecessary to hurt Mother when she would never have to know once things were set straight anyway, right? (Silence.) Attempting to encourage the response I was looking for, I asked Nedd how he and Oretta would go about making things right (his words) with the money, adding how relieved I was he was going to do the fair thing and give June and Mom their equal share. I wanted to give him an out by letting him know that we understood what had happened there and that it was an easy thing to set to rights. Surely he wasn't to blame, I said, as it was obvious to all of us the codicil Grandma had added was the fallout from an argument that was almost fifteen years old and was relevant only to that particular day and time. Relationships among all of the Clankton siblings and their mother had altered a dozen or more times since then. None of us could give it serious consideration really. Finally, I told him, wouldn't it be nice if at Grandma's passing all of you could walk away with a clear conscience and clean your slates? Put an end to all the fighting and close the books on all of those personal grievances and family squabbles? Pretending they were all going to be warm and fuzzy towards each other would have been pushing the envelope, but I thought the idea of calling a truce may be somewhat appealing. Then I leaned forward with a warm smile plastered to my face and gave Uncle Nedd's anticipated response my full attention.

I could immediately see that Uncle Nedd was reluctant to agree wholeheartedly with the words I had spoken. He began shifting around in his chair rather uncomfortably and stared down at his hands folded on the table before him, rather than looking directly at me. Then, much to my surprise, Nedd said he felt Estelle should probably receive something and he would likely give her a share of his part of the money, but that he wouldn't give June so much as one plug nickel.

Wow! Wasn't he just on friendly terms with June that very morning, the only one speaking to her and sitting next to her at the funeral?! Didn't he drive her to the lawyer's office and back and hug her when she had left Hattiesville that very afternoon?! Furthermore, he said he didn't know what Oretta would do and that he didn't have any influence over her, but he would be surprised if she shared her portion of the cash with either of her sisters.

Boy, that didn't sound anything like the guy who had made all kinds of promises earlier that afternoon about working things out fairly. It seemed I was about to learn another lesson about my colorful kinfolk. Uncle Nedd had long been one of my favorite relatives and I made a point of calling, writing and even visiting every now and then if I was in or around St. Louis. I had also stopped at his home several times with friends or colleagues during our travels across country. I had always felt Uncle Nedd cared for me, heck, genuinely liked me, but just then I wasn't so sure. It appeared that his behavior could be somewhat deceiving and may not reflect his true thoughts or feelings. Judging from his Jekyll and Hyde routine with Aunt June that day, it was possible that I, too, might be considered a bad egg where Nedd was concerned after I left his home tomorrow morning. And if that were true, you could bet Carolyn and Mother would be disregarded, as well.

Well, my head was spinning with the rather abrupt change in attitude from Nedd. I didn't feel any relief that he claimed he would share his portion of the money with Mother. For me, the issue at hand wasn't about the money itself anyway. It was about the fact that things should be equally divided among the four Clankton siblings, all things considered. The fact that Nedd felt himself in a position to decide who was worthy or not, and was choosing to cut out June, was all wrong to me. Besides, if he was just saying he would share his loot with Mother to appease me for the time being, he soon opened a window that would let himself out of any exact promise of a contribution to Mom at all. I listened in awe as Uncle Nedd began to remark upon how he was struggling with the idea that if he did in fact share the money with Estelle, he would actually be going against Grandma's final wishes. "After all," he said, "if someone leaves a will it is what they want to have carried out at the time of their death." In essence, he said he would be betraying his mother's wishes if he shared the money with anyone at all. Yeah, it looked like it was eating him up inside all right. He looked like a gambler who had just laid down a winning hand.

I tell you, I was shocked by the turn our conversation had taken. I was having a hard time believing what I was hearing. True, Nedd's theory was relevant to the extent that it covered the intent of having a will at all. In the particular and peculiar case of Grandma's will, however, it was far from accurate and could not be seriously applied by anyone with knowledge of the situation. We all knew that even if it was what Grandma had wanted at the time the codicil was written, it was carried out in the heat of battle and she would have been unlikely to feel that same way a month later, let alone at the time of her death over fourteen years later!

Furthermore, the will didn't state how Nedd and Oretta should use the money. Knowing Grandma's character, they could certainly choose to right her wrongdoing and divide the money equally with June and Estelle; help atone for Grandma's sins, so to speak. It would be quite easy for them to do as the ironic thing was none of the Clankton siblings actually needed the money. They were all fortunate enough to be in financial positions allowing them to be generous. I would have liked to have thought that even if one of them did need the money the others would be willing to divide things accordingly and help each other out a bit.

WHOAA! What was I thinking? I had gotten lost in la-la land for a minute there. I needed to keep in mind to whom I was referring. To the best of my recall, none of the four Clankton jackals had ever behaved in a gracious and giving manner toward each other, my own mother included. Why on earth should I be surprised at what was happening? I guess it was because although I had known those people and the dastardly deeds they had committed against each other all of my life, I had viewed them with wry amusement. Their colorful, and often crazy, behavior was met with eye-rolling tolerance and dealt with by simply removing myself from the situation when necessary. That had worked as a child. It had even worked for me as a young adult when Grandma was alive and kicking (literally) and the siblings were in their prime. But their mother had been buried that day. And they themselves were in various states of health. Gosh, my own mother, Estelle, was pushing eighty! I guess since at that point I was an adult, too, on a more equal footing with those folks, I began to see them for what and who they were and was viewing them in a new and most unpleasant light. Their feelings and behavior toward each other was not then, nor had it ever been, a joke or a game to them, only to me. I found that I was somewhat startled to fully realize what kind of people they really were. We were. After all, that was the family from which I came, also. Not a proud moment of revelation for me.

I knew then my attempt to have a heart-to-heart conversation with Nedd was futile. The realization of his intentions was finally penetrating my thick do-gooder head. With a sigh of defeat, I let my uncle know that he would just have to do what he thought was the right thing. Then, the rest of us would simply have to live with his decision. But would we have to live with him still in our lives? I silently wondered if I would have any relationship at all with Uncle Nedd after that night. It felt like he was weighing a relationship with me and my family against the cash. It didn't look like our side of the scale was measuring up very well, either.

As I made my way back upstairs I thought yes, indeed, there were many perspectives on "doing the right thing" under those circumstances, but I had little doubt which one my uncle would choose. When I reached the top stair landing I could hear Carolyn on the phone in her room with her husband, Gil. Although I couldn't make out the actual words, her emphatic tone told me she remained quite upset about the situation at hand. I had gone downstairs actually believing that I would acquire comfort from my uncle - that his words and intentions would allow me to come upstairs and calm Carolyn down and start to put things in perspective. Oh, I had a clear perspective on things at that point alright, but I dreaded having to tell Carolyn what my gut feeling was after having chatted with dear old Uncle Nedd.

I started to get ready for bed but thought I better check in on Mom first. Mother was already fast asleep, never knowing I had been downstairs with her brother and oblivious to all that was happening with her siblings. I crept back down the hallway to my room to find Carolyn sitting on the bed anxiously awaiting the results of my talk with Nedd. I decided to get right to the point and be blunt about my hunch. After all, a little forthright honesty would be a welcome relief to that day of deceit and secrecy. I told her she was not going to like hearing what I had to say but I thought things were going to stay just the way they were. Nedd and Oretta were going to keep the lion's share of the money and I believed we would hear a variety of pious and self-serving justifications from them as to why they deserved things to remain just as they were. I did tell her Nedd said he would compensate Mom in some way but that I didn't have a great deal of faith in his words. His behavior toward June had revealed just how little he could be trusted at that point. I told Carolyn I believed Oretta and Nedd were going to keep all of the money, under the guise of carrying out Grandma's final wishes, so they could actually feel righteous about their decision of greed.

Having said all that, I actually started to cry for the first time that day. It was really a mixed bag of emotions that started my tears flowing. I was crying not so much over the loss of my grandma, who had lived to the ripe old age of ninety three, but for the pathetic life of hatred and fighting she had led that left such a trail of hurt behind. I was crying because my mother and her siblings were of such despicable character that they would all truly choose to screw each other over right down to their own final breath of life on this earth... over a dime. Finally, I was crying over my own loss of innocence regarding the people in my family. It dawned on me that the only reason I even knew those people at all was because they were my family. Despite my former amusement at their colorful antics, I would never choose them as friends.

The magnitude of that whole event was forcing me to take on the role of a real adult with people for whom I had always just been a little girl. I was actually involved in one of their battles, not just a bystander or an observer. I was being forced to make some adult decisions myself. I knew that I could choose to disassociate myself from those people, as my brother had, as June's children had, and carry on in my life without them in it. Perhaps it was time to face up to the kind of people they really were and choose not to be like them, not to tolerate them, not to treat their behavior as amusing fodder for colorful anecdotes any longer. After forty years, would those people no longer be a part of my life? Was it time for me to walk away, too?

That night at Nedd's house was a restless one and I was anxious to leave come morning, as was Carolyn. We had decided the night before that there was nothing we could really do about the circumstances. I told Carolyn that we couldn't control Nedd's or Oretta's behavior, only our reaction to it. Our decision lay in whether or not to continue a relationship with them. We must wait and see what they do. I didn't think that eased Carolyn's mind at all as she was more of a "take action" kind of gal, but it did seem even her hands were tied at that moment. We did agree that if either of them did compensate Mother in any way financially, we would have her split that money right down the middle with her sister, June, immediately - regardless of her feelings toward June at that moment. After all, our whole point was that the issue was not about the money and not about who was fighting with whom. It was about doing right by each other, calling the feuding quits, and being at peace with each other during the final years of their own lives.

After hauling our luggage down to the front entrance of the house we met up with Nedd and his wife in the kitchen again and I was determined to be polite, despite my feelings. I thanked them for their hospitality and graciously declined breakfast by saying that we needed to get an early start to arrive back home at a decent hour. My excuse was accepted without argument partly because there were reports of possible snow along Interstate 70 in eastern Kansas and partly because Nedd was equally eager to have us depart. As we began moving our belongings outside to load the van, Donna's daughter, Tamera, came upstairs holding a CD. She was dismayed we were leaving so early as she was getting things ready in the family room so she could sing for us. Nedd, a little too eagerly I thought, said, "These people have got to get going, NOW, to beat that snow!" Okay by me. I was relieved both to get on the road and to avoid another home concert from Tamera.

Backing out of the driveway, I took what felt like the first deep breath I had taken in at least 24 hours and let it out slowly in one long sigh. I just wanted to be away from those people and use the monotony of driving that long stretch of highway to put my thoughts in order. I heard Carolyn let out a long breath also, maybe because she felt the same relief I did. Or, maybe because Mom was waving out the window inviting everyone out to Colorado that summer to visit us. Ohhhhh, another long sigh.

The drive home was a solemn one, except for Mom's incessant stream of chatter about everything from road signs to what the people in passing cars were up to. There was little else for us to do about Grandma's will except wait and see how things played out. Life would go on as usual. What had happened wasn't going to make a huge impact on our day-to-day living. I kept telling myself I would just have to make decisions as things came up, knowing in my heart that Nedd and Oretta had already made their decision and I had made mine, too. Leaving Hattiesville even felt like it might be the last time. Looking out the car window over the rural landscape along the interstate I could have been any age. I had made that trip many times and my mind couldn't help but wander back over the years to the family and events that shaped my childhood summers in that part of the country.

PART TWO

THE FAMILY

CHAPTER FOUR

Estelle

My own mother, Estelle, is the oldest of the Clankton siblings and without a doubt the most ferocious. She is also one of the only two siblings to have graduated from college and move from the state of Arkansas, June being the other. Mother married her high school and college sweetheart, my father, Galen, and moved to Colorado when I was only a few months old and my sister, Carolyn, almost four. To Carolyn and me, Colorado has always been our home state. Not so for our brother, Reese. Reese, fifteen years older than I, spent his childhood in Arkansas where our parents, just after they finished college, taught school outside of Little Rock for several years before moving to Colorado. By the time I was old enough to retain memories of my youth, my brother was out of the house and well into college some distance away. We saw little of him and as I grew older I began to understand why. He had long ago made the decision to disassociate from the family into which he had been born. He seemed to have come to an early realization that there was a more decent way of living and more decent people to live among. Reese was always an intriguing person on the fringes of my life and a bit of a mystery to me. He became less mysterious as I grew older and sought my own escape from our tumultuous home.

As it was then, in my mind, my immediate family consisted of my parents and my sister, Carolyn. Yes, Colorado was our home, where my parents worked and we girls attended school and, although we had our friends and activities to fill our lives most of the time, a year never passed without a visit to my grandparents' farm in Hattiesville, Arkansas. Carolyn and I longed to go to Disneyland, to the beach, to any place other than Arkansas. Once or twice we were lucky enough to visit the Grand Canyon or drive to Florida with our parents, but that was in addition to our annual pilgrimage to Hattiesville. There was no escaping that inevitable event in our summers. Estelle was adamant about visiting her parents and siblings, though one had to wonder why. Our time there was always pretty predictable, following a pattern of a pleasant arrival and initial comradery, the resurrection of old wounds and new jealousies, an acceleration to verbal abuse and physical violence, and the early departure of one of the Clankton siblings, quite often our mother, with my dad and sister and I in tow.

Estelle's father, my grandfather, had also been a school teacher in Eastern Arkansas for most of his life, but had settled into a retirement of farming and raising hogs in Hattiesville before I was even born. He and my grandmother, Iola, lived in a single-wide trailer next to an old farmhouse they used for storage on their place. One of their daughters, my Aunt Oretta, and her brood of five children had their farm and hog operation just a mile or so down the dirt road from them. Hattiesville was definitely hog country.

Now, although I am sure we must have at some time or another, I personally had no recollection of ever having arrived at my grandparents' farm in the light of day. It seemed a part of the expected routine that we would get there after dark, maneuvering our Buick down the muddy dirt roads in the rain. It was almost always raining during our arrival. The rain made the odor of the hog pens particularly pungent and opening the car door to that humid and foul smelling air did not exactly signal the beginning of a fun-filled family vacation. Carolyn and I usually had to be awakened in the car so that we could make a drowsy-eyed dash to the trailer house in the rain and mud. Our excitement was limited; we were usually just ready to get to bed.

The one and only small guestroom in my grandparents' trailer routinely belonged to Carolyn and me during our visits to the farm. Our parents slept on the living room sofa sleeper so they could stay up late and talk or play cards with the other adults. Our room was lined in cheap paneling from floor to ceiling, corner to corner. A sliding door in the wall closed us off from the hallway. Not that we ever used that door. We would have suffocated in that hot and airless room as it had only one small rectangular window, about 12 x 14 at the top of one exterior wall. The trailer did not have air conditioning and a fan in the hallway stirred the only breeze to be had. Carolyn and I slept together on the double bed that took up all of the space in that room except for a narrow path you could walk sideways down between the bed and the closet. We slept in thin summer pajamas on top of the sheets and still awoke clammy and hot each morning. Carolyn's face broke out into a pimply rash from the moment we arrived at the farm until we returned home, and every photo we had of those visits showed me with damp looking hair separated into stringy locks by the humidity. For Carolyn and I the humid Arkansas climate was always a shocking change from dry, relatively cool Colorado.

Overall, however, Carolyn seemed to adapt to our summer environment better than I did. She was more of a tomboy and easily knocked around the farm and adjoining woods with our cousin closest to her in age, Winnie, one of Aunt Oretta's daughters. I, on the other hand, was usually inside engaged in some quiet activity, bedecked in a Bobbie Brooks ensemble, or picking my way gingerly around the yard, knocking dirt out of my white summer sandals. The only cousin who lived nearby that was close in age to me was also one of Aunt Oretta's children, Jason, their only son after four girls and revered as something almost certainly holy. Jason and I had little use for each other. To him, I was just another girl and his superiority had been instilled in him from birth. To me, he was just a bumpkin farm boy who had poor grammar and no particular talents other than the fact that he could drive a truck, which made no impression on me. Trucks were for bumpkins. So, except for the rare occasion when Carolyn and Winnie allowed me to tag along, I simply entertained myself.

Regardless of how unappealing those trips to muggy Arkansas in the height of the summer were to Carolyn and me, our mother was in her element. Estelle was a woman of little patience and would not have tolerated much complaining from us anyway. Or from our father, for that matter. With Mother, it was always better to silently conform to whatever it was she had in mind than to cross her and suffer the wrath of her hair-trigger temper. Having said that, Dad, Carolyn and I pretty much went along for the ride, awaiting whatever form the inevitable fallout would be among the Clankton family on that particular trip.

Mother was always fairly pleasant to be around on the way to visit her family, if you could tune out her incessant talking in the car for several uninterrupted hours. Whether anyone was actually listening to her chatter or not was irrelevant. Mother wasn't necessarily speaking to any of us, she was just speaking her every thought and feeling, and reading every road sign and billboard we passed on the highway. The rest of us were all well-practiced at tuning Mom's chatter out to a sort of white noise in the background. Dad drove in silence while Carolyn and I read, slept or played a quiet car game in the backseat.

Occasionally, Mother would surprise us by expecting a response to something she had said, usually to Dad. Of course Dad, like us, had heard the noise but not attended to the words or subject matter and it was obvious that he was clueless as to how to respond. During those times, Carolyn and I would hold our breath and look at Dad with big eyes, hoping he could cover well enough to avoid upsetting Mother. When those "expected answer" situations came up we could sometimes get away with a nonverbal response that could be rendered appropriate to any topic, like a "hmmmm," or a "mmm hmmm," and Mom would then continue her verbal barrage and we could all tune back out. There were times, however, when it was clear she felt we should all have been attending to her every word the last several hours and was incensed when we couldn't give actual feedback when she demanded it. That would flame the temper that lay just beneath the surface of our mother's demeanor at all times and the talking would become more volatile, inflected with hostilities, usually directed at Dad.

If you have ever been in a situation like that, trapped into having to listen to constant talking that is anything but reciprocal, it is mentally exhausting, even when you have done your best to block it out. Sometimes Carolyn and I actually used her chatter as a source of amusement when we got really bored in the back seat. We had a game we would play when we could ignore the verbal onslaught no longer. The goal of the game was to be able to count to ten on our fingers (silently and hidden, of course) any pauses or silences between Mother's endless flow of words. It may be hard for some to believe but winning at that game was a rare occurrence. We had actually made entire trips from Colorado to Arkansas without so much as ten seconds of silence in the car. Carolyn and I could at least fall asleep in the back seat for a little respite. Not so for poor Dad, as he had to drive. Mother herself had never been known to nap on even the longest car trips. Our only other relief came when we stopped to get fuel and we would lose Mom to the ladies room for a few brief minutes. During those stops, the rest of us would drag ourselves wearily from the vehicle and stand around the car stretching. Carolyn and I were not children who whined and pestered our parents for candy and drinks. We mostly just enjoyed the silence.

Estelle's very presence was enough to create tension, whether in a car, a room, a crowd. You just never knew what she was going to interpret as a personal insult or what would provoke her to outrage. Even happy and good occasions took her emotions to such manic heights that things often ended up in verbal or physical disaster. That was true of her excitement to get to Arkansas, too. Indeed, by the time we finally arrived at the farm, Mother was more vigorous than ever as she was pretty worked up about seeing her parents and siblings. So, while Carolyn and I dragged ourselves out of the car, or were sometimes carried off to bed, Mom was just getting wound up. With total disregard to how weary my father might have been from driving all day, or to her own parents' possible desire to go to bed, having been up farming and feeding animals since 5 a.m., mother would talk and walk freely around the cramped trailer house until well past midnight. My dad's attempts to get her to bed were largely unsuccessful. Mother followed her own agenda and everyone else could adapt, by golly. She would either get mad at Dad for hinting around (Mother takes suggestions from no one) or, if she were in a pleasant, compliant mood, she could still stretch out her getting ready for bed a good hour or more, talking on and on all the while, heedless to the needs or desires of anyone else in the house.

Once we were all settled in for the visit our family rarely left the farm for any reason. Mother did not spend any of her boundless energy on Carolyn and me nor did she make any efforts to provide us with amusements or entertainment. We were pretty much left to follow our own course for the duration of our stay. Estelle was going to busy herself with her favorite activity, sitting with her own mother and whichever sibling was also there visiting, and trashing the sibling(s) that were not there at the moment.

The only real entertainment I can ever recall taking place among the adults in the Clankton family was the occasional game of pinochle. That innocent-seeming card game was dreaded by me, and all of the cousins for that matter, for the outright violence we all knew it could inspire. Estelle was way too self-involved to care about being socially appropriate and she did not take losing well at all. She was easily provoked and had been known to throw her cards at someone, even hit another family player, before leaving the table in a fit of rage. Dad once told us, years later, that before they were married, Mom had visited his room at college one evening and they had attempted a game of cards. Unfortunately, the cards were not falling in Estelle's favor that night and she got mad and started ripping the cards right in two, throwing them down on the table! The thing I found most surprising about that story was not Mother's behavior, but that Dad continued to date and later marry her. Lord, did he need a bolt of lightning?!

As shocking as her behavior may seem to some, Estelle was not the only Clankton to exhibit such wild outbursts. Aunt June could rock a card party, too, though hers was more of a sullen, tight-lipped getting up from the table with an air of superiority over the other imbeciles in the room. Also, their mother, my grandmother Iola, always did her best to incite trouble with her own style of dissension which included mumbling disparaging remarks and shooting looks of hostile accusation at the other card players. By far, though, Estelle's actions were surely the largest and most physical of the Clankton clan.

Other than the periodic pinochle games, Estelle was quite content to just talk and talk and talk with her family. It was a rare occasion for her to ever take a walk down the lane, go fishing with us, read, or engage in any other diversion the entire time we were there. She certainly never gave a thought to the well-being of Carolyn and me. Nope, it was Dad who occasionally went fishing with us, or Grandfather who would let us ride with him to the grocery store in the old pickup truck. I was always eager to go anywhere and do anything with anyone at anytime as I was so bored and lonely during those visits to the farm. As I was not particularly the outdoorsy type, I was eager to get into town, to civilization, where the fear of copperhead snakes and even tarantulas and scorpions did not lurk around every corner. Where chiggers didn't fill your socks and underwear forming their tiny itching red welts. I craved cement sidewalks and paved roads, people, shops and movie theaters. I never begged but silently hoped for a comic book and a candy bar or grape soda. I was happy with anything that might be thrown my way, sort of like a dog who was just happy to have someone pay attention to him on those trips. Throw me a bone.

As a family, we never once went out to dinner or to a movie during our time at the farm. We didn't take any day trips or venture out to visit any sights of interest like Hannibal, Missouri, just a few hours away by car, and even closer from Uncle Nedd's house in St. Louis. We could have stayed there overnight and gone back to the farm the next day. I know, because I had worked it all out. I was an avid reader as a child and would have loved to have visited Mark Twain's home and explored Tom's and Huck's old stomping grounds. There were other places I would have loved to have visited, too, like Mystic Caverns, Dogpatch U.S.A. or the Ozark National Forest. Also, I would have loved a trip to Memphis, but would have settled for a picnic at Lake Charles. With both parents being educators, you would think we might have done some of those nearby interesting things. But, no, those trips to Arkansas were clearly Mother's vacations and we were at her mercy, which meant we were on our own. So, Carolyn fished and walked the lane between our grandparents' place and Aunt Oretta's home to meet up with Winnie, while I read, colored, and made up games in the yard. In the evenings after supper I would chase fireflies in the yard to put in jars and Carolyn would sometimes join me if she wasn't going to spend the night with Winnie at Oretta's house. Not an entirely miserable existence, but not exactly an inspiring vacation year after year after year.

The one exception to being trapped at my grandparents' farm for the entire time spent in Arkansas was a quick trip to our cabin near the Black River, located just over the state line in Missouri. My parents had owned that little log cabin, The Whippoorwill we called it, for many years. My brother spent a great deal of his childhood summers there when my parents lived and taught just outside of Little Rock, all those years before I was born. During our annul trip to Arkansas we would always stop at the cabin before or after our visit to the farm, once or twice taking Grandma and Grandpa with us.

I enjoyed being at the cabin so much more than the farm. For one thing, it was our place and I was just more comfortable there. My toys and books were there and I felt a greater liberty in using my own things, getting a snack when I wanted it, etc. Also, Carolyn was more willing to spend time with me, mostly because she had no other option, I knew, but I enjoyed hanging around my big sister and tried hard to be "cool." I did not want to appear too much like an annoying little kid sister. I think Dad felt less confined at the cabin, too, without all of Mother's family gathered around us. He would take us out fishing in our little row boat, lead us on hikes through the woods, and even swim with us at the public pool in the small town nearby. Mother of course, rarely joined us in these activities, but even she seemed a little more willing to cook outside or ride into town for an ice cream with us after dinner. If Grandma was at the cabin with us, however, the two of them preferred to just stay inside and continue their verbal tirade against most of humankind.

The arrival of Mother's other siblings to the farm, or even the cabin for that matter, although it was rare that any of them joined us there, was a mixed blessing.

I absolutely loved it when either Aunt June or Uncle Nedd came, for two reasons. One, was that they were both so much kinder to me than Aunt Oretta and paid more attention to me than even my own mother, Estelle. I far preferred their company to that of Oretta's or Mother's. Secondly, they both had children close to my age and, although they, too, were all boys, they were better companions for me than Oretta's son, Jason, was to any of us. For one thing, Jason was quite full of himself as he reigned as boy king on the farm. When the other boy cousins arrived, however, Jason paled in comparison. Jason was a big fish only in the mud puddle of Hattiesville society. The children of Aunt June and Uncle Nedd were smart, witty and multi-talented in music, language and general knowledge. They held their own in the much bigger pond of urban schools and communities. They were not arrogant like Jason, however, and were always very willing to include me in their activities and conversations. Summer vacation came alive for me when any of them came to visit the farm.

The arrival of Nedd or June had a dark side to it, too. Again, Mother was always initially glad to see those other siblings but it would only take a day or two for the hostilities to build to a boiling point. Any combination of the Clankton clan could only spend a limited amount of time together before the proverbial "shit hit the fan." For Estelle, the arguments and discussions that lit her fuse may have varied a bit from time to time but they were all rooted in the jealousies and competitiveness she engaged in with her siblings. For example, she and June were sure to get into a fight as

June gave her the most competition in the "whom is better than whom" department. June was also a college graduate, teacher, married with two children and had both a nice home and a summer cabin. Mother always felt that June carried herself in a haughty manner and considered herself superior to the rest of the Clankton clan. That really got Mom's goat because, after all, that was her own role to play. Mom just hated it when June drove up to the farm in a new Chrysler New Yorker Town Car (her husband, my Uncle Lambert, worked for Chrysler in Michigan), and made Dad upgrade from Buicks to Cadillacs so June couldn't have one over on her. Though a fight between Estelle and June could be about many things, often even politics, it was motivated by a lifetime of one-upmanship and jealousy.

Now, Uncle Nedd would usually set my mother off by making light about something Mom took quite seriously. Estelle had never been known for her sense of humor but her intolerance for an opinion that differed from her own was famous. She was not one to agree to disagree, either. Estelle often did not appreciate her brother's manner of joking or trying to make light of a situation and he was occasionally on the receiving end of some inanimate object Estelle decided to throw in order to shut him up. Although I felt Nedd was the most easy going of all of the Clanktons, he would occasionally lose his temper with Estelle and mouth off to her or simply tell her to shut up. If his sister then came at him physically he usually just went outside to cool off. Sometimes that worked with Estelle; other times she just wouldn't quit and would follow Nedd outside to resume fighting there.

Estelle's anger manifested itself in loud and physical ways, usually pushing someone into packing up from their visit earlier than they had intended. It didn't end there for her, either. She was notorious for keeping up her verbal and physical abuses as people were loading their vehicles. She had run alongside her siblings' vehicles to continue her tirade more than once and had even laid behind the rear wheels of their cars in an emotional rage so that the offended party couldn't drive away. I always thought Mother really pushed her luck there as I was sure there was some temptation to roll on over her. Once a particular battle was over and someone had left in a huff, it would take several hours for Estelle to calm down and stop haranguing the departed sibling in their absence.

The day after such an episode, Estelle would go into her act of confused innocence. She just couldn't understand why Nedd/June/Oretta had acted that way. "Why are they so hateful?" she would ask. "Why did they leave like that?" The answer to such questions was always the same for Estelle - they were, of course, jealous of her. Always had been. They were nothing. They didn't have any sense, never did. In the case of Oretta and Nedd she was sure to add that they were uneducated since they hadn't gone to college. They were, therefore, just ignorant. Estelle would recruit her own mother into that train of thought and Grandma willingly joined in with her low opinion of the child that had left prematurely. Perhaps because she had started so young, giving birth to Estelle when she was barely sixteen, Grandma behaved as if she was another sibling to her children, rather then their mother. When you considered Grandma's behavior, it was easy to determine that if Estelle was a little crazy she had come by it honestly.

Not long after a Clankton family gathering ended in just such a typical and predictable feud, my family, too, would begin the long car drive for home. Now, of course, Mother would have a whole new series of thoughts to share with us in an uninterrupted verbal stream. The drive home was always a bit edgier somehow. Too much Clankton family togetherness, too much of our mother, Estelle, could try the most patient of souls and my dad would occasionally reach the end of his willingness to ignore Mother. When Dad would lose his patience on the way home, disagreeing with Mother or correcting her or, worse yet, even telling her to be quiet, it usually meant some serious fighting. We would often end up pulled over on the shoulder of the highway. I can remember Mother getting out of the car once on Highway 412, just outside of Fayetteville, while Dad sat behind the wheel of our car for a long time without moving before he finally drove up beside her and told her to get back in the car. I wondered if he had sat and fantasized for a few minutes how it would be to just pull out into traffic and keep on going without his wife. It would have been quieter, for sure.

If we stopped at a hotel for the night on the way home things could get physically violent between Mom and Dad, with Mom throwing stuff around and taking slaps at Dad. Mother's sense of drama on those occasions would go into full swing. A common scene of hers often included yelling "He's killing me!" at the top of her lungs in a hotel room while she was knocking Dad about the head and chest with her fists. Dad would have his arms up in defense, warding off the blows. Mother never relented, never backed down and never wavered in her belief that she was right in all matters. No matter whom she was fighting with, things would only accelerate verbally and physically until the offending party backed down, apologized or simply left the premises. Thus, Dad usually did whatever it took to restore peace just to get us all back home in one piece. If we were in a hotel, Dad's attempts to settle Mom down often came after an embarrassing call from the hotel manager, saying he had received complaints about the noise coming from our room.

Once we were back in Colorado, Estelle spent many hours of the next several days on the phone with her mother, Iola, and the sibling(s) with whom she was still on speaking terms. The goal of those conversations was to convince the others how right she was and how rotten the enemy sibling must be. In other words, those calls secured allies in Estelle's camp. Once the camps of a current Clankton battle were established they could remain steady for any varied length of time. It simply depended on where and when the next despicable act of greed or slander among them would take place - sometimes just a few months, other times they remained stable for a year or more. No one in that family would ever apologize for their outlandish behavior as none of the Clankton siblings, or their mother, were ever wrong. No, the camps would only change when one of them did something awful, which one of them always eventually did, and then the shifting would begin. Previously sworn enemies would forgive all past infractions in order to band together against the latest Clankton family villain.

That was the pattern that governed Estelle's life for years. When my parents finally did divorce, after thirty-three years of marriage, things did not change much for our mother. The subject of how rotten my dad was gave Mother untold hours of verbal fodder to share with her own mother and siblings. Also, she added Dad to her permanent enemies camp list and devoted a large part of her time waging war on him through personal harassment and various other amusing ways. For years Mom frequently called Dad's phone number forcing him to try unlisted numbers time and again. On one occasion Mother even took her blue Cadillac and rammed Dad's car in the parking lot of the apartment building he had moved into after their divorce. I was old enough to look for his car's paint on her Cadillac after Dad told me what he suspected. Oh, yes, Mother had devoted herself to a campaign of hate and revenge for more than twenty years after my parents' divorce. It was a sad thing, really. So wasteful.

In fact, now that she is well into her seventies and has experienced some pretty serious health complications, Estelle finds herself rather alone and wonders where her life went. The truth is, Mother has alienated herself from most of the people in her life with her hostile and grossly self-involved personality. After having lived in the same home and teaching in the same school district for more than thirty years, Estelle has no real friends to speak of. There is an old neighbor or two who call occasionally to see how she is doing or send a Christmas card now and then, but they do not seek her company. To this day, Estelle is unable to hold a conversation that is reciprocal in any way, though she remains able to talk AT you for hours. It doesn't matter anyway as she has little interest in what anyone else has to say if it is not about her. One would probably guess, correctly, that my mother never remarried. No surprise really, considering her preoccupation with making Dad's life hell rather than getting on with her own. There was also her "unique" personality to be considered. The most surprising thing of all might be that even with her temperament, Estelle managed to marry at all and remained so for as long as she did. I have never quite decided if my father was a saint or a fool.

A perfect illustration of Estelle's current outlook on life took place not long ago in the car with Carolyn and me. Our mother saw several houses flying the American flag as we drove around the city and asked us what holiday was coming up that had people flying their flags at that time of year. We explained that a lot of people were flying flags daily after the 9/11 attack on the World Trade Center in New York City to show their sadness, support and patriotism following that tragedy. Mother let out her trademark noise of disgust, "Pssshhhht," followed by a commentary of how stupid people could be. "That bombing didn't have anything to do with them; they didn't know those people. These people here shouldn't act like they care when it didn't affect them one bit. They're all nuts." It never crossed her mind that her sister June had a son, Mother's own nephew, living in Manhattan at the time of the attack and had undergone a rather frightening ordeal. Our mother has never exactly been someone you wanted to have a casual cup of coffee and a chat with.

So, things being what they were then, Carolyn and I had moved our mother so she would be living near us where we could better take care of her. We looked after her finances, health care and personal needs, and tried to include her in an occasional outing. Mother had settled down somewhat, which would be a surprise to those who had come to know her just recently, but she still complained about everything, appreciated few things we did for her and had alienated most of the residents in our town in a rather short period of time. Mother's take on the people in her new community was what it had always been for most people everywhere, including her family; they were all just ignorant and backwards. They were jealous of her. They were all nuts. "Why, they're nothin' but trash."

It is no wonder, then, that at the time of the funeral, Carolyn and I were reluctant to inform our mother that Grandma had excluded her from receiving any cash from her estate. Mom was currently disoriented enough to at least be fairly pleasant to be around. She was one apple cart we didn't want to upset right at that moment. Cowardly? Maybe. But it would get us all back home from Grandma's funeral without further incident. Besides, there would be time enough to clue Mom in on everything later as I had a bad feeling that, although the cash inheritance seemed unalterable, the resolution of how to handle Grandma's farm land was far from over.

CHAPTER FIVE

June

Second oldest in the Clankton family line-up is My Aunt June, the one Clankton sibling I always wished were my mother while growing up. I don't know that June was actually any better behaved than her siblings or if the grass just seemed greener on my mother's sister's side, but I personally enjoyed June's company the best.

Like Estelle, June had graduated from college and had made a career in teaching. She and her family lived in Detroit, Michigan. Her husband, my Uncle Lambert, was also a favorite of mine with his sense of humor and general kindness towards me. June and Lambert had two children, both boys, fourteen years apart in age, not unlike my brother and me. The oldest, Carl, was never around much and shared little in common with me due to the large gap in our ages. However, the youngest, Mark, was just six weeks younger than I and was, without a doubt, my favorite cousin. Mark was soft-spoken but very witty, intelligent and musically gifted. Although he was a far superior student than the rest of his cousins, including me, Mark never made us feel inferior in any way. He was always interested in what we had to say and what our own talents were. Mark and I got along famously and I always believed we would make a great brother and sister team.

In fact, I dreamed about being the perfect daughter to Uncle Lambert and Aunt June. June was very much into clothing and jewels and shopping and it was largely wasted on that household of males. She seemed so glamorous to me. She often said she wished she had a daughter to do things with and lavished me with attention when she was around. I knew that I was her favorite niece, too. I think my sister was too much of a tomboy and June didn't seem interested in Oretta's country girls either. I was a fairly shy and timid child, more of a girly-girl than the rest, destined to be the cheerleader rather than the athlete. Uncle Nedd had only boys, so that ruled any of them out of being Aunt June's favorite, too. I felt fortunate to be the object of June's favor and fantasized about shopping, going to lunch and having a mother that was a pleasure to be around and with whom I could talk. Oh, if June would only take me in, take me away from my own mother, Estelle, and her unpredictably wild mood swings.

Sometimes my wish even came true, for a little while anyway. When I was a little older and we were all at Grandpa's and Grandma's farm, Aunt June and Uncle Lambert would offer to take me to their summer cabin in Branson, Missouri, for a few days. I was always thrilled as I knew my mother would allow me to go. It made little difference to Estelle where I was spending my time, as long as I was out of her hair. For me, it was an escape from the smelly hog farm and my cousin Jason's attempts to lord over me. I relished the time spent with the cousin I truly enjoyed, Mark, and with a kind set of adults who actually wanted me around. Oh, it was heavenly!

Unlike the farm, I have fond memories of my time spent in Branson. That was the Branson before it became the show town it is today. I read *Shepard of the Hills* and we visited Uncle Matt's cabin and took trips on the Sammy Lane boat rides. We went to Silver Dollar City and I took my first and only, to date, helicopter ride. We fished and played in the water on the "beach" at Table Rock Lake. We cooked out, dined out and picnicked. Now that was a vacation! That was the family to which I felt I truly belonged. I always dreamed about being allowed to stay with June permanently and wondered if my own mother would even mind all that much. I could visit my parents on the hog farm in the summers. Or not.

Much to my dismay, however, June and her family did not migrate to her parents' farm every summer - at least not often enough during our visits there, in my opinion. June chose to keep herself somewhat removed from the Clankton family, wisely, and was only around the farm at all during the summer months because of their lake home in Branson. I got the feeling she came up to see her parents at the farm as a courtesy and family obligation, really, since they were fairly nearby anyway. I doubted that they would have visited the farm as frequently as they did if they lived year-round in Michigan, unlike our own family, who hauled ourselves out there annually come hell or high water.

June distanced herself in other ways, too, mostly with a sense of superiority to her siblings and parents. June and Lambert were always well-dressed behind the wheel of their new Chrysler Town Cars. They just didn't look like they belonged on the hog farm. Both of their boys were excellent students - the oldest, Carl, earning his doctorate in history, and Mark very accomplished academically and musically throughout both high school and college. June made sure that her brother and sisters were well aware of her childrens' achievements. June also had a lovely brick home back in Michigan, in addition to the lake home in Branson. Boy, that was all just the sort of stuff to make the rest of the Clankton clan burn with jealousy.

Yes, all of the Clankton's cared greatly about appearing successful and outdoing each other and June was no exception to that rule. Image mattered dearly to June and she worked hard to aspire to present herself as better than her siblings and made sure they were fully aware of it. She was successful at it, too. Even though her sister, Estelle, could match her on some levels, June just carried it off better and seemed to stay a step or two ahead of my mother. Even our cabin didn't quite hold up to June's summer home on the lake. We all even used different titles to refer to them as the former implied an outhouse and a pump for water, the latter all the amenities of home plus a lovely fishing dock and boat. I must confess, it was just that extra step up that partially appealed to me about June. I wanted to share in her lifestyle of nice homes and nice clothes and a nice family. I felt I would have been the perfect daughter for Aunt June.

One of the things that amazed me most about spending time with June and her husband was that they got along so well. Aunt June and Uncle Lambert seemed to truly enjoy each other's company. There was no fighting between them, at least not while I was there. Even though I tensely waited for the other shoe to drop... it never did. Unlike life with my mother, Estelle, it seemed that June and her family lived fairly peacefully when well away from the rest of the Clankton clan.

While at the farm, though, trouble could start with June, too. She had very strong opinions about politics, particularly regarding our country's educational system and, unfortunately, those opinions didn't often concur with her brother, Nedd's, or sister, Estelle's, views on the same subjects. Politics was the one thing that June would just not let up on in a discussion. She was a voracious reader and was a bit of a political zealot. She felt she had the inside scoop on the vast amount of cover ups, scandals and conspiracies being perpetuated by the United States government and you could not convince her otherwise. Like her sister, Estelle, she didn't give a hoot about the ideas of anyone else and chalked up any view other than her own as being misguided and ill-informed. Yes, sometimes Aunt June was just too much to take, too.

As for her relationship with her other sister, Oretta, one always got the impression of a general dislike of each other. Of course, Oretta, living just down the dirt road from her parents, married to a humorless farmer, raising five kids and slopping hogs of her own, didn't have much to hold up against Aunt June's upscale image, and that would have made my Aunt Oretta seethe with envy. Her only retaliation was to belittle June's opinions, accomplishments, education and lifestyle. No doubt, June looked down her nose with disdain at Oretta's lifestyle in return.

Even Iola, June's own mother, never expressed any real warmth toward June. No, Grandma was usually among the first to accuse June of putting on airs, of acting better than the rest of them, etc. So, whether she alienated herself or whether the others alienated her, June was sort of on the outskirts of the family. Although she had certainly been involved in her share of Clankton family disputes, June kept herself somewhat at a distance from her mother and siblings and seemed to live a relatively happy life as a result.

I was terribly saddened when June's husband, my Uncle Lambert, died fairly young. His son, Mark, and I were just starting high school at the time he passed away. I remember attending the funeral and how truly distraught Aunt June and my cousins were. It was my first experience with death and I will never forget it. I was asked to ride in the family limousine which meant so much to me. Again, I had felt I was a special part of June's family that day and gave no thought to leaving my own family behind. I sat in the front pew with June and her children. At one point, June had me walk up to the casket with her and touch Uncle Lambert's face, which didn't freak me out like I thought it would at first. I was just sad and in a state of disbelief, as I was discovering first hand what it meant to die and to have someone you loved pass away. I will never forget that day for what it meant to me in so many different ways, but mostly for what it meant to be valued for who I was and what it was like to belong to a loving family, even in a time of despair.

Just as it was no surprise to anyone that Estelle never remarried after her divorce, it came as no surprise that Aunt June did find another man. June needed and enjoyed having a partner to share her life with and I knew she would eventually find another husband. She was just too vibrant and active to remain by herself, even in her senior years. She married unsuccessfully the second time around, to a man who did not share her sense of humor and love of travel and who did not seem to admire or accept her sons. Wisely, and without hesitation, she divorced him. A third husband, Roger, has proven himself to be a kind, caring and fun loving man and they have been happy for many years now. In that way, there is a "normalcy" in June that seems lacking in her sister, Estelle. I am happy for Aunt June. She and Roger travel extensively, enjoy dancing and dining out and seem to have friends in many places. June seems genuinely happy sharing her life with Roger.

In more recent years, I had visited Aunt June and Roger in Branson and spent time with my cousin, Mark, there and at his home in New York City. June and Roger had also come to Colorado to visit Mom a time or two, most recently following her first mastectomy in Mom's fight against breast cancer. Of course, June and Mother had fallen into opposite camps since then but seemed to have now landed back on the same side in the latest Clankton battle. Who knew what the future would hold? My guess was that the reading of the will by Mr. Lawrence P. Baylor was not the final word on a subject so near and dear to June's heart. That's right. It pains me to say, that despite her decency towards me and regardless of my affection for her, June was a Clankton through and through.

Make no mistake, June, like all of the Clankton siblings, has had a keen interest in her parents' wills for many years. When my Grandfather passed away twenty years ago, the issue of his will was a huge factor in that "grieving" process, too. The Clankton clan were all gathered at Grandma's house and June, my mother, Estelle, and my sister, Carolyn, and I were spending the night there. I was a senior in high school that year and remember being just old enough to be disgusted but not surprised at the brouhaha between June and Estelle over what might be, and what certainly should be, in Grandpa's will. Regardless of the fact that they had just lost their father, completely insensitive to their mother, who was upset and in the next room, those two engaged in a shouting, slapping, door slamming spree unlike any other cat fight they had been tangled in previously. It was grossly inappropriate and proved to me that the Clankton family hallmark of selfishness and insensitivity was alive and well and thriving in the hearts of all four siblings, June being no exception.

Since then, much heated discussion had arisen from dialogue about what was best for Grandma and how the farm land should be used, sold, etc. You will recall that it was the subject of the last hostile encounter between June and her sister, Oretta. It was hard to know if June's concerns about the will stemmed from a general mistrust that her siblings would attempt to manipulate the will or if she, like the others, was inspired by greed and a need to make sure she received not only her fair share of the inheritance, but possibly more through her own scheming. After all, who was to say that June wasn't trying to sell Grandma's land during that fight she had with Oretta a few years back for her own purposes. Maybe June was trying to gain control of Grandma so she could set the money up for herself when her mother passed away. That would most certainly be Oretta's version of things, though I really couldn't say for sure either way. What I was sure of was that we would be hearing more from Aunt June, or more likely her lawyer, on the subject of Grandma's will very soon.

CHAPTER SIX

Oretta

If there was a favorite among my aunts and uncle then you can guess there was a least favorite, as well. It was no secret to anyone in the family that, for me, that title belonged to my Aunt Oretta. The first thing anyone notices about Oretta is that she is the only Clankton sibling, heck, the only one in the entire extended family at all, who speaks with a very distinctive southern accent. Where she acquired that twang is a mystery to all of us. Her husband and children do not speak that way. She has never lived in any part of the deep south where she might have adapted to the local lingo. Her parents, my grandparents, never sounded anything like that, either. In fact, few things on this earth sound anything like Aunt Oretta. Oh, make no mistake, Oretta's southern accent is not the soft-spoken, slurred type that brings to mind Scarlett O'Hara entertaining her gentlemen friends with tall glasses of iced tea sipped on the veranda. Oretta's vocal output is more closely compared to the caterwauling of some wild animal in a state of serious pain. It is a very nasal, high pitched noise and the last syllable drags out just long enough to give you the impression that she is whining with every sentence. Even when I have tried to make an attempt to be around

Oretta, all she had to do was open her mouth to remind me of just how annoying I found her to be. The odd thing about that crazy assumed accent is, I have no recollection of anyone ever ridiculing her about it, or even questioning her about it, during a Clankton family battle. That was hard to believe, really, for it was all even I could do to restrain from telling her to knock it off and speak normally for goodness sake.

Anyway, Oretta was the Clankton sibling who always had trouble presenting herself in a way that would impress, or even compare favorably to, her brother and sisters. Oretta did not go to college and did not go far from home, or her parents' home, either. Oretta and her husband, Lou, had always lived just a mile or so down the dirt road from my grandparents' farm. Oretta and Lou also farmed and raised hogs. The smell of their place alone put Oretta at the bottom of the Clankton dung heap when it came to comparing lifestyles of the Clankton siblings.

Oretta's husband, my uncle Lou, is nothing to crow about, either, in terms of education, sophistication, witty banter or even interesting conversation. Lou is a close-mouthed and severe looking man. Tall, thin, balding and clad in denim overalls he is American Gothic come to life. Lou is a man with a "king of the castle" mentality and Oretta had spent a lifetime shuffling around Edith Bunker-style attempting to meet his domestic needs. Together, Oretta and Lou had five children: four girls and one much revered boy (you remember Jason, boy king). I knew for a fact that they would have had less kids altogether if a male child had arrived sooner in the line up. I had little doubt Lou would not stop having children until the almighty male heir to the hog farm was born. Oretta would, of course, have had no say in the matter herself. Not that it would have been an issue for Oretta anyway as to her, too, males reigned superior.

Much to her great dismay, Oretta did not live in a particularly nice house compared to her sisters, either. She raised her five children in the old three-bedroom farmhouse on their place and Lou's mother lived in a single-wide trailer in the back yard. Now, Lou and Oretta did own a fair amount of land and it was the one thing Oretta could feel good about pointing out to the rest of the family. In fact, Oretta would drive us around their place, point out the window and say, "That's all our land, as far as you can see. Just as far as you can see." The phrase never varied and her words became a sort of mantra of self-esteem building for her and we had heard it repeatedly over the years. It was all she had to offer, really, in the comparison and one-upmanship event held annually by the Clankton siblings. It was really rather awful that, even as adults, we had ridiculed Oretta behind her back by repeating that phrase, mimicking her irritating accent, and laughing. As little as I cared for her I did feel kind of bad about that. Kind of.

As far as any actual Clankton family battles went, Oretta was not the most volatile of the group. She was quite adept at engaging in disparaging remarks about an enemy camp sibling, but often did so in a less obvious way. Yes, Oretta took the prize for the most devious, underhanded, behind your back perpetrator of the four siblings. Her style was to remain quiet until the enemy was gone and only then did she participate in tearing them down. She was not one for direct confrontation and it gave her a sneaky edge. It was sometimes difficult to know which camp Oretta was in and thus, she was not to be trusted at any time. Often, after she had engaged in a devious act against another Clankton sibling, she simply remained quiet when she was confronted and it made you very wary. One did not assume Oretta's silence implied innocence. It would be wise to keep one eye on that snake in the grass as her bite was unpredictable.

Oretta's primary way of dealing with her jealousy of the other siblings was also carried out in very passive-aggressive ways. For example, it irked my mother and June, and even Nedd, that Oretta would not visit and, indeed, had never visited any of her siblings at their homes, despite the fact that they all came to visit in Hattiesville regularly. She was always invited to their homes or cabins but in more than forty years, Oretta had never darkened any of their doorways. That was really no surprise to anyone as we all knew wild horses couldn't drag Oretta into the yard of one of her siblings nicer homes. It would have killed her to have to actually look at their brick homes, nice cars and more affluent lifestyles. Oretta had no interest in getting into that kind of comparison contest with her siblings. As long as she had never seen their homes it was all just heresay as far as she was concerned and she did not have to face up to any superiority on their part, or inferiority on hers. I thought if you were to have put Oretta in the yard of one of her siblings' homes she would have melted into the ground just like the Wicked Witch of the West.

A few years ago, however, Oretta and Lou finally built themselves a ranch-style brick home on their farmstead, just up the hill a few hundred feet from their old farm house. Putting that home in was Oretta's grandest day. In her mind, she had finally arrived and could hold her head up; she now had air conditioning, new carpets, cement sidewalks. Her need for approval from the rest of the family, however, had turned Oretta into the Minnie Pearl of home furnishings. If she could have left the price tags on or taped the bills of purchase to certain items in her home, she most certainly would have. However, even Oretta knew that would be overdoing it a bit. Instead, she made it a point to single out certain items around her house, then told you outright how much she paid for it or said things like, "It was the most expensive one they had," or "Don't say anything to Lou because he had a fit over how much it cost." Those desperate and humiliating attempts to impress, combined with her unwillingness to visit or acknowledge anything her siblings had, were a living testimonial to just how deep the competition among the Clankton siblings ran. Oretta's whole life had been mired in jealousy and insecurity. I could almost have felt sorry for her, if I hadn't known her so well.

Now, one might guess that Oretta's need to gain some standing in the Clankton family ranks extended to the children, also, and they would be right. Oretta's children versus the rest of us cousins. Although she was unlikely to confront any one of her brother or sisters directly, she had little restraint when it came to saying belittling and derogatory comments to their children. That behavior included Nedd's and June's children as well, but it seemed that early on Oretta had developed a strong dislike for me. Oretta seemed to focus on making my life particularly uncomfortable by pointing out things I couldn't do, acting shocked by it and making me feel inferior to her son, my cousin, Jason. Jason and I were only six weeks apart in age so to Oretta and my mom, Estelle, it was an ongoing struggle to prove whose kid was better overall.

For Oretta, it was a huge point of pride that Jason could drive a truck at age ten, as many farm kids tend to do. Unfortunately, Jason did not have many other claims to fame and it was a sore spot with Oretta. Oh, and you could bet on the fact, Estelle made sure Oretta knew that over the years I had been an academic honor student, in the band, was head cheerleader, editor of the school newspaper, and took piano lessons outside of school. Compared to Jason I looked like a child genius. Actually, the truth of the matter was that Mark, June's son, ironically also six weeks apart in age from Jason, was the truly talented one. Heck, even I paled in comparison to Mark, but I loved him dearly and admired his outstanding qualities. Not so for Oretta and Jason. Mark was a gentle and intelligent boy, very unlike Jason's rough farm boy demeanor, and that alone gave them fodder to scoff at what they felt was Mark's "femininity."

As for me, Oretta's only recourse against my mother's bragging was to make me look, and subsequently feel, bad about myself. Her own daughters were well-instructed in the kitchen (that's where girl's belong, you know) and she often loudly expressed disbelief that I didn't know how to make deviled eggs, or some kind of Jello salad or another, and at my age, regardless of what age I was at that time. "Good Lord, Libby! Hasn't your mother taught you anything yet?" she would screech. She made it known just how lacking she thought I was because, despite my academic accomplishments, what good was a girl who didn't know how to fry bologna by the time she was in the fifth grade? Golly, I remember feeling deep shame, about deviled eggs in particular, while I was at the farm, but I seemed to forget all of my terrible shortcomings in the kitchen once we returned home and I got involved in my regular activities.

Other than the land she and her husband owned, and the exaggerated accomplishments of their only son, there was one other thing of which Oretta had always been proud, and that was her membership to the local swimming pool in Hattiesville. Oretta treated that little cement square of water located in the corner of the town's public park as if it were an exclusive country club membership. You see, it was not a public swimming pool, but was for members only and we could only go as guests of Oretta's family. Now, for years I didn't really get that whole setup and had no idea what was behind all of those rules. I was stunned when I was about junior high age and my sister, Carolyn, told me that the whole point of the "members only" policy was to keep out the few "colored" people who lived in that county.

That was a shocking piece of information to me at the time. That an entire town would band together to discriminate against a group of people based on the color of their skin was incomprehensible to my naive way of thinking. Where were we, for goodness sake? I just couldn't believe my ears! My family lived in a sizeable city and went to school with and associated with folks of all colors. Gosh, my gym teacher at school back home was black and was the best athlete I had ever known of any color at that point. Did those people mean to say that my gym teacher wouldn't be allowed to swim in their pool? Because he was black? Mr. Cramer was a fabulous swimmer and diver, better than anyone I had ever seen at the Hattiesville pool. I realized, too, that my gym teacher was likely more educated than most of those folks, as well. I lost my desire to go to the Hattiesville pool after that, regardless of the heat and humidity. I was, in fact, ashamed to have gone there so often, swimming in privilege.

I was not surprised, however, that Oretta and her family supported that pool with their lifelong membership. She had talked about how it was a nice, clean, family pool where they kept out the "local trash." I had no doubt Oretta would consider herself stationed far above Mr. Cramer, my gym teacher. Little did she suspect that I felt exactly the opposite. If it were up to me to weed out the "local trash," there would have been some dry summers for my Aunt Oretta and her family.

As I became an adult, Aunt Oretta and I had not created a spot in our hearts any warmer than the chilly corners we had when I was a child. She made no attempt to hide her low opinion of me and my own dislike for her was thinly veiled behind surface politeness. We had not seen each other often in recent years and there was no love lost between us. It seemed Oretta had little tolerance for me as an adult, too, as my mother, Estelle, had rubbed in her face my Master's Degree, professional position, various travels, etc. The only time any of those nice things about my life mattered to my mother was when she could throw them in the face of one of her siblings, to make herself look good. However, mentioning my unmarried and childless situation would cause even Mother to turn on me like a rabid dog.

Oh, yes, Aunt Oretta looked for things to condemn me for and when she didn't find them she was willing to ad-lib. It really bugged her too, for example, that I did not have children. I was married for five years after college but did not have children before getting divorced. That was incomprehensible and altogether unforgivable to Oretta. To her, bearing children was a woman's duty and the only reason a woman would get married in the first place. Furthermore, it had been over ten years since my divorce and I had not yet remarried, nor had I gotten knocked up. Oretta did not understand any of that and had therefore informed several family members that I was a lesbian. I learned that interesting bit of information from my niece, who had overheard Oretta discussing that possibility with my mother, Estelle. That made me chuckle because, when I was out of college and started doing some traveling around the U.S., Oretta had put the word out that I was a tramp. It seemed Oretta could create slander for almost any course I took in life.

What I found ironically humorous was that she just loved my sister, Carolyn. Oretta and Carolyn clicked like June and I did. Now Carolyn, too, was married and divorced the first time without having children. However, Carolyn went on to marry again... and again...and again. In her fourth, and very likely final, marriage Carolyn was the mother of two, and hopefully soon three, children: two boys of hers from previous marriages, plus the baby she hoped to have with her current husband in the near future. That would make four marriages and three children for Carolyn.

Now, spelling it all out like that might make it seem as if Carolyn was the family tramp. Not so. My sister is an educated and intelligent woman... who has made some very poor choices in husbands. Not this last time, though. I could see that Carolyn had finally put her business savvy and common sense to work when she chose her current husband, Gil. She had clearly learned from her past mistakes and had made a solid and wise decision in marrying Gil. He was a smart, educated, caring man who loved and accepted both Carolyn and her children. So, even though she was on her fourth husband, Carolyn was also hoping to have a third child; a marital record of which Oretta could therefore approve. In Oretta's mind, Carolyn was at least trying to do the things a woman was put on this earth to do - take care of a man and raise his children. So, although Carolyn had taken a much rougher road in life and had a wildly more colorful background than I, it was all okay by Oretta. I, on the other hand, though happy and independent and, by the way, heterosexual (but please don't tell Oretta), was met with tight-lipped disapproval.

In looking back on all that I knew about Oretta and her style of attack, it was no surprise that things had gone down the way they had with Grandma's whole funeral and will fiasco. After all, one could guess that Oretta was silently passionate about her mother's will, especially where the farm land was concerned, as she and her family had the most to lose - namely, all that farm land income they had assumed from her parents' place for years. It was certainly in character for Oretta to do something as devious as take Grandma in and manipulate her into writing a codicil to Grandpa's will. It was her style to patiently wait it out, over fourteen years, never letting on to anyone what she had done, content in the knowledge that she would get the last twist of the knife in her sisters' backs when all was said and done. She would show them all! She would triumph! Queen of the dung heap at last.

CHAPTER SEVEN

Nedd

Last, but far from least in the Clankton sibling line-up, is my Uncle Nedd, probably the most charismatic of the group and certainly the most colorful in that cast of characters. For me, Nedd had always been fun to be around both during my childhood and as an adult. The baby of the family, Nedd had always been easy-going, up for a good time and quick with a joke. His arrival on the farm in Hattiesville was always much anticipated by me. His laid back style and sense of humor made him a pleasure to be around. Plus, he had twin boys, my cousins Jimmy and Johnny, who were great playmates despite their being a couple of years older than I. Jimmy and Johnny were bright, intelligent boys heavily into music and acting and endowed with their father's jovial sense of humor. Like June's son, Mark, those cousins also readily included me in their adventures around the farm as they, too, found cousin Jason's arrogant attitude tiresome and unfounded.

Yes, when Uncle Nedd arrived he lightened up the mood of the Clankton clan in general. For awhile. Oh, initially, everyone was glad to see him and appreciated his lackadaisical demeanor. But it was just that very attitude that ended up getting him into trouble with his three sisters. The problem was that Nedd's laid back attitude carried over into all aspects of his life, including work. Or the lack of it. Despite the great hopes that my grandparents had put onto their only son, Nedd had always been a bit of ne'er do well. Nedd wanted to do well, he just didn't want there to be any work involved. Much to the dismay of his parents, Nedd never went to college. Instead, he chose to set out to make his fortune. Unfortunately, he seemed unable to stick to one particular job for any length of time. Nedd didn't want to make his fortune so much as he wanted it to land in his lap, preferably while he was lounging around pool side somewhere. King of the get rich quick schemes, Nedd was always looking for the fast and easy dollar, but never finding it.

In fact, the only money that he ever seemed to be able to tap into came from his parents' pockets. More than once they provided financial backing for one of Nedd's many moneymaking ideas. My grandparents never seemed to give up on Nedd, always believing he would do them proud in the end. In their eyes he was the golden child, their only boy. And boy, oh boy, did that set his three sisters off! They all worked hard to acquire the rather nice lifestyles they had. Even Oretta and Lou had their farm and land to show for their labors. But nothing those girls accomplished could capture the interest of their parents quite like Nedd's next business venture could. It led to some serious battles among the siblings and their parents. For one thing, it frustrated his sisters that his parents continuously lined Nedd's pockets, when Nedd had little to show for it.

Attempting to pay back the money was not a concern of Nedd's at all, either. He took their financial support as his due. After all, his parents went into those ventures as his "partners." If the money was lost, well, that was the risk involved in such business deals.

An even greater irritant to his sisters than the cash flow, was the fact that all of his parents' rich and fertile farmland was available to Nedd if he would just settle down and work the land with his aging father, preparing to eventually take over operation of the farm. The land, the income, the offer was all in place if Nedd would just quit messing around and get down to doing an honest day's work. His sisters didn't even seem to dispute the idea of Nedd's inheriting all of the land if that was to be his livelihood. It was hard to understand how he could turn down that offer at times when he had no job and no prospects. Except, Nedd was just downright lazy. He had other ideas of living and had no intention of dirtying his hands doing manual farm work. That would be way too much hard labor and it did not evoke the lush, impressive lifestyle he so desperately sought. After all, there is no such thing as valet parking for tractors.

Nope, being a farmer would have meant giving up to Uncle Nedd. He would do almost anything to avoid that pitfall in life. And he did. Nedd's low-key work ethic landed him in a variety of low to moderate income jobs, as well as in prison. That's right. Nedd's desire to make fast money with little effort tempted him into a position peddling drugs. Unfortunately, he proved he wasn't even a very adept criminal. He was caught early into his life of crime and spent a few years in the state penitentiary. It appears he was nabbed by the authorities while attempting to deliver a truckload of marijuana to a distribution center of sorts.

The most amazing thing about that whole situation was that it didn't lower my grandmother's good opinion of her baby boy one bit. Grandma consoled herself by telling us all how well he got along with the prison authorities. She was impressed when Nedd told her they referred to him as Mr. Clankton, as she took that as a sign of respect. My grandfather had already passed away by the time Nedd landed in prison and that was a good thing, I thought. It would have been a bitter pill to swallow to know your only son thought so little of the land that you worked so hard to acquire, saving up from your teacher's salary, working it in the summer months until you could retire and farm it profitably, that he would rather risk running drugs illegally than to follow in your footsteps.

Although I personally always enjoyed our occasional encounters with Uncle Nedd and his children, his personal life was as puzzling to me as his professional life was to the adults. For instance, although I can describe Oretta's husband, Uncle Lou, and can give you details on Uncle Lambert, June's husband, I never really associated anyone with Uncle Nedd. Not even the twin's mother, my Aunt Patricia. Oh, I do recall seeing her around once or twice but, in my mind, Nedd sort of stood alone. Perhaps his personality was large enough to eclipse his spouse. I knew, however, that Nedd's personal life also had some real life mystery and intrigue about it. For example, he did have a son, older than the twins, that I had never met until Grandfather's funeral when I was a senior in high school. I was stunned to see how much that older, formerly unknown cousin looked like my own brother, Reese. I guess I expected him to be a total stranger but I could have picked him out as a Clankton on a crowded sidewalk anywhere. I liked that cousin, Steve, when I met him, too, but to this day don't really know who his mother is.

I didn't know, either, if Nedd and Steve's mother were ever married or not. I did know that Nedd divorced Patricia at some point but I was not aware of exactly when that happened. I didn't really notice when she stopped being around as I couldn't recall being much aware of her at all. Of course, kids can be like that where adults are concerned. Too young to know or understand the details of grown-up lives. During my years in college I was aware, however, that Nedd was living with (married to?) a woman from St. Louis and I knew she had serious health problems and had passed away. By that time, I was at an age where I was wrapped up in starting my own adult life and I didn't fully grasp all that was going on in Nedd's personal life. Regardless of his current situation, I was always happy to stop and see Uncle Nedd when I was traveling back and forth from Wisconsin home to Colorado during my college years.

A few year's ago Nedd met and married a new woman. It turned out to be the best thing he had ever done. Finally, lady luck had smiled upon old Nedd and her name turned out to be Donna. Donna was an only child of wealthy parents, both aging and ill. Not only was she loaded financially, but Donna was also a lovely and warm human being. I felt she was a great addition to the Clankton family and I liked her immediately.

Nedd and Donna made quite a striking couple largely due to their, well . . largeness. They were both quite overweight, obese really, and were rather showy in their attire, so it was not surprising that they drew a lot of attention to themselves when in the public eye. They both had a fondness for gold jewelry and on most days were just dripping with it. Donna was a very attractive woman whose hair, make-up and nails were always immaculate. Uncle Nedd was less debonair but had a penchant for multiple gold chains and rings, including the dreaded pinky ring. Unfortunately, they both also had a myriad of health problems including diabetes, respiratory difficulties, back pain and so forth. It may be that their health problems had contributed to their weight problem, but the reverse seemed more likely.

It appeared Nedd had met the perfect match in Donna not only in terms of lifestyle but in work ethics, too. From what I had seen, they just didn't do much. Or move much. Neither Nedd nor his wife worked. They seemed primarily to live off Donna's parents' money. Any other source of income was unknown to the rest of the family. During my visits to their home it appeared their lifestyle consisted of sleeping in late, dining out and hitting the casinos around St. Louis each evening.

There was no doubt that, as a result of that union, Nedd's life had greatly improved and he seemed to have finally found happiness. For one thing, Donna's parents came to live with them in St. Louis so their daughter could assist them in their senior years. Now normally that would not be an ideal arrangement for most marriages. However, Donna's parents purchased an expansive three story home in an exclusive neighborhood. That place had so many rooms and amenities that a person could go for days without seeing another occupant of the house. The third floor was exclusively for guests, while the main level housed the bedroom suite of Donna's parents. Nedd and Donna occupied the master bedroom on the lower level. Both couples had complete kitchens on their floors, as well as living room space and private outdoor entrances. Not too much chance of feeling overcrowded in that home.

Their sprawling abode was beautifully decorated, too. It came that way. Home decorating would have been way too much work for Nedd and Donna. The house was no bother to maintain, either, as Nedd and Donna had help that came in weekly. There was a woman to do the laundry and a woman to clean the house. Donna's back would not permit her to tackle either of those tasks. Gosh, just ascending the stairs from their lower level living quarters to the main floor left both Nedd and Donna winded. One could not imagine them attempting to drag cleaning equipment from room to room on three different levels. There was also a service to care for the lawn and landscaping. Considering his size, I would guess Nedd might risk a heart attack if he attempted to mow in the heat and humidity outdoors. Besides, pushing that mower might have been a bit too reminiscent of farming.

I had always enjoyed staying with Nedd and Donna and had stopped there on several occasions while traveling by myself. Their daily routine was always a source of amusement to me as it was so different than anything I had ever known. To begin with, Nedd and Donna had three little dogs that were the most pampered, revered animals I had ever seen. Those three pooches were, of course, professionally manicured and groomed regularly and sported little colored bows around their ears and tails. They were also clad in frilly little doggie diapers, called Bitch's Britches, that were worn at all times while they were in the house and removed before they went outside to relieve themselves. The appearance and treatment of those mutts never ceased to amuse me.

While a guest in Nedd and Donna's home I would expect to be taken out for any meals I would be eating with them. Of course, there was the exception of prepared foods that were brought in from restaurants or delis, usually for lunchtime meals. I had never seen anyone make anything other than coffee in either kitchen in that enormous home. Now, that was not to say that the dining out was fabulous by any means. Nedd and Donna's taste for food was far from gourmet and instead tended to lean toward filling and plentiful. Most often, they seemed to dine at buffet-style establishments, like Ryan's or Golden Corral or Ponderosa. Chinese buffets were also popular with those two. Making a run for fast food of some kind was often their source for late night snacks.

Once, I actually did have breakfast in their home with them. Or it might better be referred to as brunch, because by the time everyone had assembled in the kitchen it was about 10:30 or so. Being an early riser, I had been upstairs in my suite quietly reading for hours, trying not to disturb the household, when I smelled coffee brewing and went on downstairs. I could hardly restrain my disbelief when I saw that the kitchen table held mounds, and I mean literally piles, of fast food breakfast items. Someone had made a run to McDonald's and had now created a breakfast buffet of sorts with wrapped danish, McMuffins, breakfast burritos and hashbrowns. They must do that fairly often as it seemed like no special deal to Nedd and Donna or her parents, so I simply grabbed a burrito and a cup of coffee and joined in the feast. When in Rome, you know.

Despite the frequent consumption of somewhat less than healthy foods, Nedd and Donna did show some concern for their health problems and must have been aware that their weight only compounded their difficulties. Not long after they were married they acquired five or six exercise machines and set them up in their basement. They were more like exercise beds, really, and they had acquired them from a local massage therapist or chiropractor or specialist of some sort. The beds were designed to provide a form of nonimpact, low joint stress exercise, ideal for people with severe weight problems. Well, Nedd and Donna both easily weighed over three hundred pounds and it seemed to me that at least it was worth a try.

I tried out each of the beds myself and it sort of cracked me up the way you just lay down on the well-padded surface, flipped the switch and let the machine move your body. One of the beds lifted each leg up and down alternately. Another slowly twisted me in the middle left, then right. A person wouldn't even have to be awake for this! The machine would just manipulate your body while you rested. I thought it appeared to be the ideal workout for the likes of Nedd and Donna. It was the most inactive attempt at exercise I had ever seen. I was not sure what happened to those beds, though, as they were nowhere to be seen the last two times I had been in their home. Maybe they found that the machines were not beneficial to them or perhaps even that little bit of exercise proved too much effort for Nedd and Donna and they simply got rid of them. The latter was more likely and it seemed Nedd and Donna had not replaced them with any new form of exercise and, as a result, they continued to struggle with obesity and related health problems.

Considering their somewhat odd but rather lavish lifestyle, it was hard to imagine why Nedd would be stingy with the comparatively small inheritance being left by his own mother. It would appear he was in an exceptional position to be generous to his sisters. But appearances can be deceiving and recently there had been some family rumor and speculation that Donna's coffers were approaching empty and things may no longer be so financially rosy for Nedd and Donna. It seemed that they may have over-extended themselves in that department and that only their debt was in the six figure bracket. That might explain Nedd's interest in once again looking to his own parents for financial assistance. I know it would never cross his mind that he had been given far more than his fair share of his parents' money over the years while his sisters had received nothing. No doubt, if he was in financial trouble he would take Grandma's crazy codicil to heart and use it to help bail himself out yet again. After all, Nedd was the only son. He was only taking what his mother wanted him to have. Heck, if you considered that his parents had offered him the whole kit and kaboodle more than once, he was even being shortchanged on what he could have had. He was getting what he was rightfully due, even less than that.

Boy, what I wouldn't have given to have just been a kid again, unaware of the true characters of the adults in my family. Ignorance was bliss by comparison.

PART THREE

THE FEUD

CHAPTER EIGHT

The next few months offered little change. Once home, Carolyn, Mother, and I all carried on with the daily doings of our own lives but there were still conversations about what was to happen with the final settling of the will. Equitable division of the money was still up in the air as Uncle Nedd continued to declare that he was going to share his portion with Estelle, but not with June. Nedd said he was even going to drive the money out to Colorado personally and visit a little at Mother's new home. That was okay by me, as I knew that any money my mother received from Nedd would be split evenly with June. Both Carolyn and I would see to that as we still cared little about the actual money but wanted to attempt to set things in order where we could.

Aunt Oretta, on the other hand, had sent only one communication since dropping Mom off at the Hattiesville diner - an email to Carolyn stating that her lawyer, the honorable Mr. Lawrence P. Baylor, naturally, had said she was due some form of monetary compensation for taking care of Grandma during her final years. Clearly, Oretta was running her own defense and rationalizing to us all why she should keep all of her fifty percent of the cash - it was due her for services rendered! Now, the way she was making that sound you would think Oretta had perhaps taken

Grandma into her own home those last few years, feeding, clothing, even bathing her. Not so. Grandma had never lived with Oretta nor was Oretta ever personally responsible for her care. It was true Oretta had taken on the role of overseeing Grandma's nursing home care over the years. She lived closest to her mother and things sort of naturally fell to her by proximity to the situation. But it didn't cost her any sleep, extra laundry or cooking detail, nor did it cost her a dime. Grandma's money paid for her own health care services and nursing home stay.

Now, some might say, yes, Oretta was due some slight compensation for overseeing those arrangements for her mother. Others might note that no compensation should be due for doing what was decent and right regarding the care of your elderly parent, especially when there were no costs to you beyond time and perhaps a little mileage. And yet others might be interested in the fact that throughout the twenty some odd years after Grandpa died, Oretta's family had and still was farming her parents' land and assumed all profits personally. That alone was not bad financial compensation for visiting a nursing home once a week. Additionally, once Grandma had been place in an assisted living facility, and later into a nursing home, no one had seen any of Grandma's personal belongings. Not one scrap of furniture, glassware, jewelry or any personal effects other than clothing, seemed to exist. When asked directly by her siblings about their mother's belongings, Oretta had given vague and ever-changing answers as to their whereabouts. To this day, no one seems to know if Oretta sold everything and kept the money, or whether she had distributed the items among her own children, keeping several precious things for herself.

So, while Aunt Oretta was busy painting a benevolent picture of herself to Carolyn, I was still on speaking terms with Uncle Nedd. Although the proper distribution of the money relied on the ethics of Nedd and Oretta to do the right and gracious thing, the will did state the land itself would have to be dealt with equally among the four siblings. Once again, as the executor/guardian, Nedd took on the role of peace keeper, assuring us all things would be dealt with fairly. He comforted us with words of having the land appraised, listing it with a realtor from Little Rock or Memphis who would have a broader advertising base, hopefully selling it at or close to the appraised value and dividing the money four ways equally. We were placated by his words, although somewhat warily, as it at least seemed Nedd was trying to do something right. I still wanted so desperately to believe in him.

Quiet and seemingly removed from all of that was Aunt June. I knew she had left Hattiesville furious at Oretta and wary of Nedd, but I didn't know what course her wrath would take, and she was giving few hints. June had called me only once to say she was getting a lawyer, not to appeal the cash inheritance stated in the codicil to the will, but to monitor her interests in properly selling the land. She felt sure Oretta would connive a plan that would allow her and Lou, or more precisely their son, Jason, to acquire that land at little or no expense to themselves. She felt Nedd, too, would be showing interest in the land for the first time in his life but that he was likely to focus on how quickly he could liquidate it into cash and may take the first willy nilly offer thrown his way. But, since Oretta was smarter and more cunning than Nedd, June figured the land would end up being sold at public auction on the courthouse steps in good old Hattiesville, right across from Lawrence P. Baylor's office. In that small town, where everyone knew the Clanktons, no one would bid against Oretta's son, Jason. After all, it was his grandparents' land, and he and his dad had been working it for years. Who among the local crowd would dare to bid on that land and still hope to maintain a decent social standing in that closely knit community afterward? Not that Aunt June was against her nephew, Jason, getting the land. In fact, she told me she felt Jason was the most obvious candidate to end up with the land, but he should then make an offer to the rest of the aunts and his uncle to buy it from them. After all, he wouldn't have to put up his mother's quarter share, so it would be a good deal for him even at a fair market price.

What a revelation! And an obvious solution. That made perfect sense to me. My cousin Jason could put an end, a peaceful end, to the entire situation by making an offer to his aunts and uncle that was fair and in keeping with the land assessment. The only problem with that happening in reality, of course, was that Jason had never taken a step or opened his mouth in his entire life unless he had prior authorization from his mom and dad to do so. Oretta and Lou had ruled Jason's life from the time he was born. As a child, their doting gave my cousin an air of superiority. As Jason grew into adulthood, however, their attentions to his every action became cloistering, even debilitating. He was desperate for their approval in all things and afraid to make a move without their prior consent. Almost as quickly as I was elated by the thought that Jason could offer a peaceful resolution to the issue of Grandma's land, my hopes were deflated. I knew in my heart the one person who could step forward and resolve our mess with honor and dignity didn't have the guts to carry it out. My cowardly cousin would await instruction from Oretta and Lou, as always.

As it turned out, June was quite right in getting a lawyer to represent her interests. What happened next was an unexpected turn in the situation. Far from receiving an offer from cousin Jason to buy the land, it was Uncle Nedd who contacted us with a proposal for the four Clankton siblings to put the land in a government conservation program that would be a more profitable venture in the long run than selling the land outright at that time. Well, Carolyn and I were skeptical but foolishly still believed, or at least wanted to believe, in Uncle Nedd enough that we said we would consider it, but we were unsure about that idea and asked if written information on the program could be provided. As it turned out, we didn't need to consider that option too long as Aunt June made it clear that she didn't have any interest in the conservation program and absolutely would not cooperate with that plan. She did not care to engage in any long-term business deals with her brother and sisters and, really, who could blame her? She had definite reasons not to trust them and just wanted all family matters resolved as soon as possible. She questioned why the land still hadn't been appraised. In fact, she was now going to hire her own outside agent to have the land appraised so it would not fall into the hands of yet another Hattiesville insider who may work for the interests of Oretta's clan, quite like the lawyer, Lawrence P. Baylor, appeared to be doing.

Well, I felt that one phone call from June was enough said on the conservation program concept. In my opinion, if any one of the Clankton siblings was against that government program it put an end to the issue altogether. Not so for Nedd and Oretta. We soon received legal notice that those two were taking June to court, hoping to manipulate her into complying with placing the land into the government conservation program they were pushing. And, they took the liberty of listing Estelle as a plaintiff along with them, although our mother hadn't even been informed about their proposal and Carolyn and I had made our stance clear after June gave it a thumbs down. It seemed their strategy was to show the court how the conservation program was the most profit-bearing use of the land and, in the long run, was for the financial good of all four beneficiaries.

I could not believe what was happening and neither could Carolyn. Nedd and Oretta were going to attempt to get a court ruling that would force June to place her share of the land in the program and, furthermore, they had wrongfully assumed that our mother,

Estelle, was going to agree to go along with their proposal. Outrageous! Didn't they understand how wrong that was? And what on earth gave them the idea we would endorse forcing June to do something she was so clearly against? Carolyn and I decided a phone call to Uncle Nedd was necessary. It turned out to be our last.

When asked about the court order, Nedd readily assumed we were calling because we, too, were upset with June for fouling up the plan. He was clearly under the impression that we would be throwing Estelle's quarter of the land into the ring with Oretta and him. He was speaking as if we were obviously advocating the same things and that June was holding "us" back. He said he couldn't understand why June was being so difficult, as the conservation program was the best thing to do with the land for all of "us."

Now, I am the one who usually keeps a level head and discusses things calmly, but even I couldn't hold back that time. I said, "No, Nedd, it isn't the best thing. Not if any one of you is against it. June certainly does not feel it is in her best interest to go along with you. You and Oretta are cheating her out of Grandma's money and you wonder why she doesn't want to be bedfellows and business partners with you?! Look, you came up with an idea that required cooperation from all four of you and you don't have it. End of story, end of plan. Furthermore, to list Mom along with you and Oretta as a plaintiff was very assuming and just plain wrong. We only agreed to look at information on the program, which you never sent. Don't you get it yet? Everyone would need to agree to place the land in the conservation program for Carolyn and me to allow Mother to go along with that plan. We certainly would never advocate forcing anyone into it. You should not be doing that either, Nedd, and I don't think the law will back you on it. There's been enough hurt and wrongdoing. June was among the injured of the siblings by the will. Enough is enough. No need to kick your sister twice, for God's sake."

Well, I can tell you, Uncle Nedd was shocked at receiving such a strong retort from the baby of the Clankton family. There were a few moments of silence over the line. Finally, he said again they were "pushing June into the program because it would bring them all the most money. It is solely for the money." That time the silence was on my part. Another moment of revelation. It was boldly evident that cold, hard cash mattered more to my uncle than anything else in this world. So much so that it was inconceivable to him that it wasn't the case for everyone else on the planet. After all, he was a Clankton and that particular familial characteristic of greed was what had brought them all to that point in the first place.

I felt a need to speak what was on my mind and in my heart at that point, and I guessed, correctly, they would be my final words to Uncle Nedd. That time, I found I was more saddened than angry when I said, "Well, Nedd, not all things are about money and not everything is worth the price you pay to attain it. These are lessons one would think you, of all people, would have learned by now." Silence once more. Click. Dial tone. I had tread upon sacred ground and denounced the almighty dollar. I thought to myself that we could safely kiss goodbye any share of Nedd's money that Estelle was possibly going to receive. And, with that final phone call to Uncle Nedd, the camps were then set, allies and enemies clearly defined. It would be Oretta and Nedd against June and Estelle. Except that time around, playing the part of Estelle was really me and my sister. I was nervous about engaging personally in a Clankton family battle. I didn't think I had what it would take to make a very good warrior.

After the phone conversation with Nedd, Carolyn and I called and informed June of our position on the proposed land program and said Estelle was wrongfully listed as a plaintiff. As far as we were concerned, at least on that issue, June's lawyer could represent Estelle's interests as well. Carolyn and I chose not to take Mother all the way back to Hattiesville for the court hearing, trusting that June was adequately prepared to defend our mutual position in that matter. Therefore, we soon received the results of the court date directly from June and her lawyer. The outcome was mixed. First, we learned the court had declared in favor of June, citing that all beneficiaries of the land would have to agree to the use of the land if it went beyond having it appraised and listing it to sell, as outlined in the will. Since one sibling was against that proposal it would need to be disregarded. Besides, the conservation program proposal involved a long range profit outlook and, considering the ages of the oldest beneficiaries (Estelle and June), it was not something the court felt would necessarily be the best use of the land anyway.

True enough. I was glad with the outcome of that situation, but I thought it was shameful Nedd and Oretta had to learn in a public courtroom what was common sense and decency to most people.

However, on a rather unexpected note, we were informed that the judge did decree the land would be appraised and sold at public auction on the steps of the Hattiesville courthouse on March seventeenth - just weeks away. Also, the auction would have to be posted publicly prior to the date of the event. Not that a public notice in that part of the country meant too much. The Hattiesville newspaper had a limited readership area, to say the least. People learned news at the local coffee shop days before it came out in the weekly newspaper around there. So, to print a public notice in the Hattiesville paper and in the next little town or two over was like shouting fire after the house had already burned to the ground. Everyone would know the land was going up for sale and there was little reason to go the auction, as young cousin Jason would be buying it and getting it cheap, too. No one would bother to bid against him since it was his grandparents' land. It appeared as though Oretta would triumph yet again. It seemed June had been right.

Carolyn and I felt removed from the courthouse events by distance and by Mom's inability to know what was actually taking place. It was a bit late in the game for a lawyer but we could continue to lend June and her lawyer our support. June's lawyer sent a copy of the court-ordered advertisement Nedd and Oretta ran in the local newspapers about the upcoming auction.

We were shocked to see the notice of the sale of the land was written without mentioning either Oretta or Nedd. The ad made it look as if those two had nothing to do with the legal mess all of that had become and the fight over the land was between the two outsider sisters: Estelle Forester et al versus June Bergner, was how the notice was written.

I had no doubt Oretta and Nedd were attempting to make it look to the local crowd like their two sisters were creating all of those problems rather than solving things peacefully within the family. Listing the sale in such a way also made it clear that my aunt and uncle, through my cousin, Jason, were free to bid on the land and would indeed be doing so. Carolyn and I hated to think the land would go up for sale on the Hattiesville courthouse steps with a good ol' local boy holding the auction, while a multitude of members of Oretta's and Nedd's families stood ready to watch the big non-event take place. The two Clankton siblings doing all of the dirty deeds had turned things around to make themselves look like the good guys. It appeared Oretta and Nedd were going to acquire the land cheap and come out smelling like roses to boot!

That was the final straw for my sister, Carolyn. Buddy, her fire was lit! Carolyn immediately decided the very least we could do was run our own ads to attempt to interest buyers from outside the immediate area. With relish, Carolyn created new ads for the land auction, listing Nedd and Oretta as the sellers in large bold print and placed it in the local newspapers in that area, as well as in larger towns, including Little Rock,

Memphis and St. Louis. She even paid for the ad to appear in a few interstate farm publications. After the ads were placed, we both felt at least something had been done and we were hoping the notices might bring forth outside buyers who didn't know or care about the Clanktons and would, therefore, bid without influence. It wasn't much, we knew, but we felt a bit better for the time being, anyway.

As it turned out, our ads did catch the eyes of a few folks. Even those of Oretta and Nedd. Not that either of them was speaking to us directly by that time. But, they still had their puppet mouthpiece, our cousin, Jason, available to work for them. It was just three weeks before the auction on the courthouse steps, almost a full year after Grandma's funeral and the reading of the will, and we were hearing from Jason for the very first time. I knew my Aunt Oretta was behind the call because Jason had dialed up Carolyn. I could have told Oretta that alone was her first huge mistake. But, because Oretta had always liked Carolyn and disliked me (the lesbian and/or tramp), I had little doubt it was she who planned to have Jason make his appeal to Carolyn. Oh, how little she really knew my sister. If you are looking for a level head at a time of emotional distress, it does not sit on Carolyn's shoulders. Oretta had unknowingly sent Jason directly into the maw of the lion.

Jason had called Carolyn to make an offer all right. Oh, not an offer to buy Grandma's land at a fair price from Estelle, but to give us a final opportunity to join in buying the land with him, his parents, and Uncle Nedd. You see, Oretta and Nedd were planning to buy the land and put it in the government conservation program themselves. Did we want to go in on it with them, Jason wanted to know? He said it would be a good deal and they were anticipating getting the land for very little money, as no one was expected to bid against them at the land auction. If Estelle, our mother, went in on the purchase with them, he continued, they would only have to pay June one-quarter of the selling price since the rest of them were all owners anyway, as the beneficiaries of Grandma's land.

Carolyn, still calm but working up steam, asked if notices of the auction had been run? Jason said Oretta and Nedd had run them in the Hattiesville paper and in the next town over. Also, he said, someone had called Oretta and reported larger ads had been placed in some other papers and they figured June had probably placed them, but they weren't too worried. The auction was set for a weekday and those usually weren't as well attended as a Saturday auction would be. "It should be pretty quiet that day and the bidding process should be short and sweet. We'll make an opening offer and it will probably be accepted right off," Jason said casually.

My goodness, could he really not see, or did he not care, that they were still attempting to short change June by not having to pay her the proper value for her quarter share of the land? He was saying outright they would get the land for way less than it was worth at the auction rather than offering her a fair price and just buying her out. As far as I knew, June was still willing to sell the land. She just wanted it done fairly, of course. Didn't they know that? Ah, but that would not be the

Clankton way. Pass up an opportunity to make a buck AND cheat a sibling? Never!

Well, let me tell you, Carolyn let Jason know just where she stood on the subject and he must have been quite surprised. Obviously, Oretta had underestimated Carolyn's feelings on that subject and had assumed her position to be more neutral than it was. Having been on the receiving end of my sister's verbal stick a few times I can tell you it can be quite a beating. As her sister, I knew what to expect. However, I imagine it scared our poor, timid, cousin half to death. Needless to say, their conversation ended with Jason hanging up on a verbal tirade of insults from Carolyn the likes of which he was unlikely to have heard in awhile, at least from a grown woman. Even if he could have gotten a word in edgewise, I doubt he would have been able to muster any defense for his actions anyway. I didn't think Jason could tolerate much conflict. He was much too insecure, was used to taking orders from his parents, and was a people-pleaser to the core. It was no surprise to me, then, when all was said and done, that round went to my sister.

After she paused for breath long enough to discover that Jason had indeed hung up the phone while she was midstream in her verbal assault, Carolyn called and told me what happened and suggested I try talking to Jason, as she had just gotten too upset. No kidding. When Carolyn is distraught, she doesn't always acknowledge what the other person is saying as she has no interest in hearing them out or allowing them to explain themselves once she has formulated an opinion.

She is only interested in giving people a piece of her mind and letting them know how strongly she has judged them to be wrong; being always right herself, you know. And, I must admit that on that occasion, from the little she did get out of him, it appeared Jason probably deserved what he received.

Despite that fact, I did attempt to call Jason back right away that evening. I wanted to know what he really thought about the whole Clankton family affair. I wanted to discuss, not scream, my concerns with him about that whole business. I wanted to know why he didn't just offer a fair price to June and Estelle long ago, or even at that late date, and be done with it. Would he, like his mother, really take pride in knowing he gypped a couple of his old aunts out of some money? I had to know. I called back unsure if he would speak to me, knowing that he must be quite shaken up after being on the receiving end of Carolyn's outrage.

After several rings, Jason's wife, Rhonda, picked up the phone. I greeted her in a normal tone of voice and explained to her how Carolyn's emotions were running pretty high, but I was interested in speaking to Jason and hearing what he had to say. I told her I was able to speak calmly and would like to see if we couldn't perhaps clear up any misunderstandings. Rhonda seemed to be a neutral party in the whole mess and was quite friendly toward me, actually. Of course, Rhonda had her hands full being Oretta's daughter-in-law, married to the crowned jewel of that family and considered not worthy of him, and one wouldn't assume she would be in on her mother-in-law's scheming.

After hearing me out, Rhonda politely excused herself for a moment while she filled Jason in on my request. When she came back to the phone, she informed me my cousin was in the bathroom with the door closed and was too upset to come to the phone. I told her that was too bad, but I understood. I left my phone number in the event he should want to speak with me in the next day or two.

I never heard from Jason. I guess he figured you only put your hand on a hot burner once to know you didn't want to try it again. Besides, the auction for Grandma's farm land would be over in three weeks and Jason could just get back to what he does best - farming the land.

CHAPTER NINE

Given a chance to brood for a day over Jason's preposterous proposal and the plan that Nedd and Oretta had for practically stealing the land back from June and Estelle, Carolyn was worked up into such a state she started conjuring up ideas on how to stop that latest injustice from occurring, even if it meant halting the auction altogether in some way. My thought was that if June and her lawyer were unable to do anything about the situation up to that point, we had little chance of having any effect, short of burning down the Hattiesville courthouse on the eve of the event. The sadistic gleam in my sister's eye at that comment made me a tad nervous. I mean, hey, I too, was pretty upset and disgusted about what was happening. Of all the things Jason could have done to resolve that mess, he instead called three weeks before the auction, doing his mom's dirty work, engaging in a plan to get the land away from his aunts for a pittance of what it was worth. The only thing they all cared about was setting themselves up to make a profit. That they would be doing so at the expense of other family members was beside the point to that pack of vultures. Oh, yeah, I was frustrated by it all, too. But doing something drastic, and maybe even illegal? I had to keep a level head lest things get way out of hand. Not that criminal intent and police involvement was entirely unheard of in a Clankton family scrap, but I had no intention of stooping to that level myself.

To make matters worse, Aunt June phoned me a day or two later saying her husband, Roger, was not doing well and was scheduled to have surgery in a few days. She would need to stay home and take care of him and would not be able to attend the auction at all. Still, she would send her lawyer to represent her best interests but knew there was little he could do at that point except give her a firsthand account of events after the fact. June sounded defeated and said she guessed Oretta and Nedd would walk away with everything and nothing could be done about it. She was not going to trouble herself further as the welfare of her husband's health was much more important than the land or the money or anything else. "It really puts things in perspective, Libby," she said.

I must admit I admired her position to back out of our family's latest feud and apply her attentions and efforts to matters closer to home and heart. At least June had the sense to know when to call it quits. She wasn't sending either of her sons to the auction in her place or leaving Roger in the care of someone else so she could attend herself. She was willing to let it all go to focus on the things that were truly important in her life. I told her I respected her decision and hoped the surgery went well for Roger and to let us please know how he was doing. And that, as they say, was that. June was off of the front lines and out of the latest Clankton battle altogether.

Once again, my sister and I were left feeling helpless. What could we do, within the confines of the law, that would have a chance of changing the course of what was going to take place in just two weeks now? I asked Carolyn if she thought the ads she had placed would bring in a diverse group of people who would be both interested in bidding on the land and ignorant of our family squabbling? Were the ads enticing enough to make it worth the drive to the anything but fabulous town of Hattiesville? "After all," I said, "we want them to think they could get such a deal on this land that it's practically being given away!" And that's when it hit her. Right at that moment a light bulb went on inside my sister's head and it made her laugh out loud!

"That's it, Libby!," Carolyn hooted, "We CAN give them something for free! We can make the drive to Hattiesville very much worth the trip for people. We can put on a free ham and bean feed to get people to come to this auction! The bidding starts at 1:00 p.m. so it's a perfect set up for a free lunch. What do you think?" she asked me with excitement.

Well, the idea gave me quite a chuckle, too. "Wouldn't that be something?" I said. After all, we knew how people in our own community turned up at the fairgrounds or community building when there was a free barbeque or chili supper to be had. Why, you're sure to see folks you've never seen before and many you had not seen since the last free feed. It made you wonder what those people did with their lives between free meals. Yes sir, there was no doubt, free food was a drawing card. And ham and beans would be just the ticket to get people in that part of the country to line up for a taste. I shook my head, chuckled and said, "Yes, that would be a doozie all right!"

Then I saw from Carolyn's expression she was disappointed in my reaction. I was treating the idea as an amusing thought and she was absolutely serious about carrying out such a farce. "Come on, Libby," she insisted, "I mean it. We can do this. We have all of the equipment we would need. It would just be ham and beans, cornbread and drink coolers of iced tea. We'll run new ads, bigger and bolder than before, to let people know. We still have time. We'll do all of the cooking ahead of time here. The bread will be fine for a day or two and we'll keep the ham and beans in huge plastic bags in coolers on dry ice. People do that all the time camping. We can take the roasters and run extension cords from the courthouse an hour before we start serving to warm the food. We'll get ice in Hattiesville and just make the tea when we get there. There are already picnic tables in the park in front of the courthouse so we'll use a couple to serve off of and the rest can be for seating. It's not going to be that hard. Let's do this, Libby. We will at least have tried to do something about this abominable situation."

Always a worrier and ready to analyze things down to the last detail, I was concerned we would probably have a good turnout of people for the free lunch, but wondered if anyone would be there to actually bid on the land? After all, the fair sale of the land was the whole point of our getting involved. Carolyn convinced me that, although we would have no way of knowing who would be there for the food and who would be there for the food and the auction, it would be worth it to see the look on Nedd's and Oretta's faces as they drove up to the courthouse. Now, that was true. Those two were hoping to quietly, quickly and cheaply obtain Grandma's land on a sleepy Thursday afternoon in Hattiesville. Now the day would be a free for all, literally, and their plan just may be foiled if an unexpected outside person or two actually did have an interest in buying the land.

I confess the idea had begun to grow on me as I lay in bed that evening. It was true, we would at least be doing SOMETHING. We would be standing up and taking action where we saw a gross injustice about to take place. It really wouldn't be too difficult to pull off, either. Carolyn and I had done a little catering over the years and we did indeed have all of the equipment we would need to feed a couple hundred people or so. We had served more than that at weddings and conventions on occasion and had no problems. One had to consider, however, interfering with the auction like that would forever put a chasm between us and the rest of the Clankton clan, with the possible exception of June. However, it was probably safe to say there would be little or nothing between us after all that had happened already anyway. Smiling up at the ceiling, I thought it sure would be an interesting way to spend our next and truly final trip to Hattiesville. The free feed would be our going away party when you looked at it that way. That time it was me who laughed out loud and I decided to tell Carolyn first thing in the morning that I would do it. Now, all I had left to worry about was ensuring that we handled the food properly during our excursion so we didn't leave a little farewell gift of botulism to the good people who were going to be eating our ham and beans.

The very next day I helped Carolyn devise an ad that made it look like a regular circus was coming to Hattiesville on the day of the auction. And it sort of was. In addition to the free food, we thought it would be fun to offer pony rides to the kids who might show up. We figured it would give us more room in the vehicle we drove if we used Carolyn's horse trailer to haul catering equipment. What gave us the idea of taking one of Carolyn's boy's ponies was the catering equipment only used up one side of the trailer space. Heck, we had gone that far, we might as well go all the way and invite people to bring the whole family! We also discussed offering face painting and bringing in a local band to provide live music but we thought we better not get too big for our britches. We settled on throwing in the portable sound system we had used at several parties in the past, along with some country and western cd's we thought would please the hog raising, farming population that would be in attendance.

The one thing still bothering me was that we could be going to all of that trouble and even have a good turnout but it still didn't guarantee that Nedd and Oretta would have to pay a fair price to their sisters for the acquisition of the land. I could see Carolyn was getting frustrated with my fussing over that little detail. She told me in an exasperated tone of voice that there was just no way to guarantee that anyone would bid against our cousin, Jason, unless we did it ourselves and we certainly didn't want any farm land in Arkansas.

Now, that thought stopped me dead in my tracks. Could we bid against them, I wondered? Oh, not to actually buy the land. It was true, we didn't want it. We didn't even want to keep Jason or any of the rest of the family from buying the land. We just wanted to ensure that someone pay a fair price to obtain it. But, could we bid on the land during the auction just to drive up the price? We would have to decide just how much we wanted the land to sell for based on the assessment from the land agent so we would know at what point we wanted to drop out of the bidding. Whichever one of us did the actual bidding would have to be very careful not to forget we were not in the auction to actually acquire the land. The bidder could not get wrapped up in their emotions and get carried away and bid wildly for the sake of revenge on Nedd and Oretta.

Well, that certainly left Carolyn out. No way was I going to turn that emotional wild card loose in the auction process. She could work up steam like a runaway train and there would be no stopping her. Carolyn was likely not to give in on the bidding until WE were the ones buying the land, and probably at an outrageous price above and beyond what we hoped someone else would pay. Heck, it could end up that Oretta and Nedd would make a nice profit on the land by giving up the bid to us! No, Carolyn needed to stick to dishing up the free food.

That still left us with no one to bid during the auction. I was also excluding myself as a candidate for that job, of course, as I was as equally inappropriate for the task as Carolyn. I was afraid I would have just the opposite reaction to being involved in the actual auction. I would be wracked with anxiety going into the event and may start to second guess the whole plan during the process. What if I backed out of the bidding? For one thing, Carolyn would kill me as she had little patience for weakness in a person. Bidding on the land was just too personal for me, too, and I was not confident I could keep my own emotions at bay. We needed a more neutral party, but who? Our brother, Reese, would be a great choice as he would go in, do the deed and never bat an eye. He was removed both physically and emotionally from our family and it wouldn't effect him one bit. Thing was, Reese kept himself removed by not getting involved and I knew he would think anything to do with the Clankton clan wasn't worth one minute of his time. So, back to the drawing board.

Now, about that time, as Carolyn and I were poking around her kitchen getting out baking pans for cornbread and figuring out the list of ingredients we needed to buy, in walked Carolyn's husband, Gil, for a cold drink and a quick sandwich before he went back out to the field on the tractor. Of course! Why hadn't that occurred to me before?! Gil was the perfect bidder for our auction. He was part of our family, true, but he had little to do with the extended Clankton clan as he had come into the picture fairly late, when he married Carolyn a couple of years ago. And, Gil was himself a farmer of sorts. Oh, he hadn't always been a farmer. Gil left his parents' farm and ranch after high school and went on through college to earn degrees in engineering and economics. He had spent the bulk of his adult life, before his marriage to Carolyn, living in San Diego and working for an engineering firm.

A few years ago, however, Gil made the move back to Colorado to help his aging parents run their place. Gil missed the city life and particularly disliked the few cattle he worked for his father, but the farming he didn't mind so much. He actually kind of enjoyed working the land and had remarked more than once that he could be happy doing a little farming in his retirement years if he could cut down on the acres and get rid of the cattle altogether.

Gil was smart. He was knowledgeable about farm land. He was level headed. He was perfect. Gil would be our bidder. I sat my sister and her husband down at the table and told them how I thought Carolyn's statement of bidding on the land ourselves could be put into action. We hammered out the details over our sandwiches (tuna, not ham) and sodas.

CHAPTER TEN

Carolyn, Gil, Mother and I left for Arkansas early the day before the auction was to be held on the courthouse steps in Hattiesville. We had the food, all of the serving equipment we would need and, of course, the pony and its feed all packed up in the horse trailer. Carolyn had arranged for her two boys to stay with the families of friends for the two nights that we would be gone since her husband, Gil, would be coming with us. I was responsible for preparing Mother for the trip which turned out to be a fairly simple task. A day or two earlier Carolyn and I had sat down with our mother to attempt to inform her of what was taking place. We decided to leave out the part about her own mother excluding her from receiving anything directly from the monetary portion of the estate. Mother had yet to catch on to that little detail and we couldn't see how pointing it out to her would serve any purpose but to cause her additional grief. After all, her mother was no longer of this earth and there was no opportunity for the two of them to settle the issue in an invigorating round of insults and accusations. Better to leave her with fond memories of her mother than to hurt her with the truth.

Instead, we focused on what was happening with the sale of Grandma's land. We were truthful about what Oretta and Nedd were trying to do and told her of our plan to manipulate the auction a bit. Needless to say, Mother was all for it. It was, after all, another chance to embroil herself in a feud with her siblings and she stood to benefit financially, a combination no Clankton could resist. It rather disturbed me that Mother, even in her state of reduced health, could still rally at the thought of getting one over on her brother and sisters. For that was how she perceived what we were going to do. It was very much a "let's get 'em" attitude on Estelle's part. We had difficulty making her see that we weren't out to actually harm them or treat them dirty, which she was clearly gung-ho about. We tried to explain that we were simply going to force all of the Clankton siblings to play, and pay, fairly. We were wasting our breath. Mother relished the thought of a good old family showdown. She was more excited than we had seen her in years. That was, when she could even remember that we were going back to Hattiesville and why.

I had been concerned throughout the whole process of settling Grandma's will that we hadn't really informed or involved Estelle. After all, it was her mother and it was her land and her siblings that we were dealing with. Leaving Mother out of the loop had been eating at me a little bit the last few days. It felt sort of like going behind her back. But, witnessing her reaction after we filled her in on things, I felt good about the fact that our decision to take action had little to do with Mom. I fully realized then that I was not involving myself in that circus to champion my mother in any way. I harbored no delusions that Estelle wouldn't be just as capable of planning some ill deed to cheat her siblings out of the land and money were she in full swing. No, I was hoping what we were about to do would be a lesson to them all, my own mother included. We were taking a stand for equity and fairness, decency and good. I wasn't sure any of them would ever see it that way but, at the time, I believed we were doing the right thing. We were taking action to prevent evil. It felt like the stuff of super heros. Fighting for truth and justice… with ham and beans.

The drive to Hattiesville was fairly uneventful. We were all pretty worked up, excited and anxious about what was to occur the following day. We talked over the details as we drove to make sure everyone knew their part. When we stopped for a quick bite of dinner at a fast-food chicken place just as we crossed over the state line into Arkansas, I asked Carolyn if she were at all nervous about the next day. She said she hoped we had brought enough food to feed everyone and that the pony wouldn't buck anyone off. Yes, but did she still feel we were doing the right thing, I wanted to know? Carolyn replied that we were indeed doing the right thing as Oretta and Nedd needed to be set straight and, besides, Mother was not able to protect herself against her siblings and it was up to us to look out for her best interests.

We looked over at our mother who was waiting in line for the restroom with dentures in hand, using a fingernail to clean out the bits of extra crispy chicken that had gotten wedged in between the teeth, enjoying the last tasty morsels of her meal. From the disgusted look on Carolyn's face I think at that moment she, too, was having second thoughts about going to all of that trouble for any member of the Clankton clan, even if it did involve our own mother. I again had to remind myself that we were getting involved because it was the right thing to do and that we would have taken action against Mother, too, if she were trying to wrong her siblings regarding Grandma's will. Then why was I feeling less and less like a super hero all the time? Did Superman ever feel that maybe he should just let some people get what was coming to them as just desserts for their own bad behavior? How about Spiderman? Did he really believe everyone deserved to be rescued, regardless of character? I was starting to think maybe I was just not cut out to be Wonder Woman.

We spent the next hour driving to our hotel as night fell outside the vehicle windows. The talking and excitement from earlier in the day had dissipated and Carolyn, Gil and I drove along without speaking much. The long day of traveling and the anxiety I had been feeling was starting to wear me out. That, and the fact that Mother, who was sitting in the front seat next to me while I drove, had not quit talking since we left the restaurant.

We had made hotel arrangements in a town several miles away from the courthouse to avoid early detection from any of our relatives, so we ended up driving right through the heart of Hattiesville under the cover of darkness. As we passed the courthouse, I was thinking how different it would look tomorrow with all that was about to take place. That nagging anxiety I kept feeling surfaced again. I would be glad when the whole thing was over and we would be driving our rig in the opposite direction toward home.

Gil and Carolyn sat quietly in the back seat and I imagined they, too, were exhausted from the trip and were thinking about the day to follow. I caught Carolyn's eye in the rearview mirror and raised my eyebrows, giving her a look that let her know Mother's incessant dialogue was making me weary. She nodded her agreement then turned to look out the window into the darkness. I decided to spend the last miles to our hotel amusing myself the way I had for almost forty years. Each time Estelle paused in her speaking I began counting to myself. We didn't have a full ten seconds of peace until we got Mother settled into her hotel room and closed the door behind us. Only then could we each retreat to the blissful silence of our own rooms. Tomorrow was going to be a long day and I wanted to be rested and prepared to make the best of it. In all of my usual worrying I had lost sight of the fact that it was supposed to be a fun day where good triumphs over evil. After all, we were only doing good things - feeding people, giving pony rides, and seeing that the land sold at a fair price. With those positive thoughts in mind, I was able to drift off to a fitful but fair night's sleep.

We arrived at the courthouse early the next morning to set up for the free ham and bean feed. Carolyn was going to oversee the food but it was pretty much set up to be a self-serve situation. The folks in the courthouse were very good about allowing us to run electricity from the building to keep the ham and beans hot in our roasters. Gil was in charge of the pony rides as I am afraid of all horses, regardless of their size. My job was to keep the music going, pour cups of iced tea, keep an eye on our mother, Estelle, and watch for Nedd and Oretta and their families to arrive.

A good crowd began showing up around 11:30 and, much to my relief, things went quite smoothly. Folks seemed happy to be picnicking out on the courthouse lawn on that fine spring day and there were a few children there too young for school who were thrilled with the pony. I found myself able to relax and even enjoy myself a bit. Carolyn is great at talking and joking around with strangers and, as people came through the food line, she was putting in a good word or two on behalf of the farm land, encouraging the people who were interested in bidding and generally making everyone feel right welcome.

By 12:00 noon there was still no sign of anyone related to us in the crowd. I didn't expect Oretta and Nedd to actually come and get in line for the vittles, but surely they couldn't resist seeing what was happening on that most important day. I knew they couldn't hold out too much longer and I was right. At 12:15 they came. They drove in procession with Oretta and Lou leading the way in their new Lincoln. Nedd and Donna followed in a new gold Cadillac that made me think they had already put the inheritance money they had received from Grandma to good use. Jason and his wife, Rhonda, were next, and I saw one or two of Oretta's girls following behind in their cars. I gave Gil a thumbs up to signal their arrival and walked over to where Carolyn was still serving ham and beans.

Since the food line was down to a few stragglers by that point, I was able to pull Carolyn aside and face her toward the parking lot where our kinfolk had just parked their cars. I couldn't wait to see the look on Nedd's and Oretta's faces when they got out of the car. I must admit, I was looking forward to that moment of revelation and wore a big, smarmy grin on my face. After all, the free feed had drawn a good turnout of folks and things were going as planned so far. I wasn't to be disappointed, either, because as our distinguished relatives got out of their vehicles it was clear when the moment of truth hit them right between the eyes!

Oretta got out of her car first and slowly looked around the courthouse lawn. It took her a few minutes to locate the food table but I knew the very instant she made eye contact with Carolyn and me that she was truly shocked to see we were the rascals behind all of the commotion. She turned back to the cars and informed Nedd and Donna and her own husband, Lou, about who was to blame for the interference in their plan. I could tell from the looks on their faces, as they, too, located us standing smiling at them from the crowd, that they truly had no previous notion we were the ones behind the scene of all that lay before them. Clearly, they had seen the ads and knew about the events that had been arranged to promote the auction, but they must have assumed June was still responsible for all of the antagonistic opposition taking place. We knew from Carolyn's previous phone conversation with Jason that they had assumed June had run the first ads and Carolyn never got to correct him by telling him we were the ones who had spread word of the auction outside their own county lines. It seemed they had then attributed the later ads and the free lunch offering to June, too. They knew we had turned down Jason's offer to bid with them to get the land away cheap from June, but they never guessed we would try to stop them altogether.

Well, I'll tell you, I laughed right out loud! It was a priceless moment. Don't get me wrong. I wasn't exactly laughing at my relations in a mean, vindictive way. No, indeed. I was laughing at the beauty of how well our plan had all played out. I did feel like Wonder Woman at that moment and the bad guys were getting exactly what they deserved. No one was getting hurt, no one was getting cheated. Everyone was simply being forced to engage in fair conduct. Oh, Nedd and Oretta would be very angry at not being able to steal the land for a song from June and Estelle. But that was okay. The bad guys always got angry at having their evil plan foiled by the super heros. I looked over at Carolyn to slap her on the back and congratulate her on coming up with such an ingenious plan, only to discover that Carolyn wasn't laughing.

The look on Carolyn's face wiped the grin off my own. The only word to describe what I saw there was rage, pure and raw. Far from seeing the amusement in what was happening before us, Carolyn saw nothing but her own contempt for those people. And, just at that moment, before I knew what was happening, she was off. Carolyn took off across that courthouse lawn like a rabid dog and headed directly for the parking lot where our relatives were standing. I headed after her and could hear her shouting even over the country and western music that was still playing for the picnickers. She yelled at Nedd, asking him if he had bought his @*%#! new Cadillac with the money he swindled from his sisters?! She cursed Oretta for being so @*%#! petty and insecure that she had never visited her siblings' homes in her whole @*%#! lifetime!!

Nedd and Donna were already heading across the street in the opposite direction and they picked up their pace quite a bit when they heard Carolyn coming. It seemed that group had made plans to meet in the offices of their lawyer, once again, the infamous Mr. Lawrence P. Baylor, which turned out to be a good thing, really, as it seemed they would indeed be needing a refuge of sorts. Jason and the rest of our cousins were already in Mr. Baylor's office and only Oretta lagged behind to engage in a bit of verbal battle with my sister. I heard Oretta shouting at Carolyn, asking her what did she think she was doing, coming around there making trouble, as her husband, Lou, was taking her by the elbow attempting to steer her safely across the street and into the lawyer's office. Once Carolyn realized our relatives were all headed inside the building she stopped charging and yelling and I was able to get her headed back up on the lawn and focused on the task at hand. We had to clean up the serving equipment and get the pony tethered to the trailer before the auction began. We went about our duties silently, as Carolyn still looked tight-lipped and furious, and I was recovering from my own shock at my sister's unexpected behavior. It seemed this time, I was the one who had underestimated Carolyn's feelings

By that time, my own feelings of light-hearted amusement had dissipated and I now had grave concerns that the day could turn into an ugly public brawl among the warring Clanktons. The very thought of that happening knotted my stomach muscles into a ball and I felt sick with anxiety. I was determined some level of civility be maintained between our feuding families so, as we neared the end of the clean up, I told Carolyn I wanted to speak directly to Jason as he was the one that was likely to be doing the actual bidding on the land. I felt I would like to let him know up front what our intentions were by being there that day and going to all of the trouble we had. I wanted someone from that side of the feud to understand that even now, the issue at hand was not about money to us and we were not out to stop them from getting the land. We didn't want to swindle them, but we were not going to let them cheat anyone else either.

I also wanted to let Jason know that I couldn't understand why he hadn't just offered his aunts a fair price for the land in the first place and avoided all of the trouble. I still wanted to give him a chance to explain himself, I guess. Or, maybe I was really wanting to justify to someone my own reasons for being involved in the ordeal. Either way, now that I was knee deep in the whole mess, I wanted to carry out our mission with honor, decency and truth. Carolyn said she, too, wanted to hear from Jason and wanted to come with me when I spoke to him. I let her know that I wanted to speak with him calmly, like reasonable adults. Carolyn said she would be quiet and let me talk, so I agreed to let her come with me. What was I thinking?

Together we walked across the street to Mr. Baylor's law firm. I passed through the small waiting area with Carolyn close behind me and stood in the open doorway of the office where all of our relatives were seated and engaged in a heated discussion about why Carolyn and I were in town and just what we planned to do. The conversation came to an immediate halt as everyone in the room stared expectantly at me. I spoke in a very courteous tone when I said, "Jason, I would like to speak with you alone, please. Privately. Outside."

It was, of course, Aunt Oretta who spoke up right away, telling Jason not to go. Well, that set Carolyn off again and she let loose with another string of insults to Oretta and threw in a few to Uncle Nedd, too, about his drug dealing and prison time. Needless to say, Jason was not eager to come outside and who could blame him. Carolyn was starting to make a nervous wreck out of me, too, and I turned around and told her she needed to leave. "I want to speak to Jason and you can't handle it, so you need to go back across the street. Now, please."

Carolyn, being the older sister and all, was not used to taking directives from me and I thought she may just blast me with a few words, too. I was much relieved, then, when she did back off and walk over to the courthouse lawn to join up with her husband, Gil, and our mother, Estelle.

I took a deep breath, gathered my courage, and walked back into the office and appealed to Jason once again to please come outside and speak with me. I told him Carolyn was pretty distraught but I was okay and would like to speak to him privately without any yelling or insults. I then looked right at Oretta before she had a chance to say anything and said, "I'm talking to Jason and he can probably make his own decision on this simple request." And, much to my surprise and relief, he did. Jason got up and headed toward me and the door and we walked out of that office, leaving the rest of the Clankton clan sitting in bewildered silence. We found a spot a few yards down the sidewalk from the legal office that offered both shade and privacy. We just stood with our heads down, shuffling our feet for a few moments, collecting our thoughts and our breath.

When I was ready to speak, I thanked Jason for walking out of there and meeting with me. I told him I felt badly things had gotten to that point between our respective families. He said he felt the same way. Having mutually acknowledged the situation had gotten ugly on the Clankton front, I slowly began to explain why we were there. I told him that the land was going to sell that day for the fair market value as determined by the appraiser. Period. "Now," I calmly said, "you can buy the land, we can buy the land, or someone else entirely can buy the land. We don't care who the buyer is, we only care that it sells for a fair price. There are no land deals or steals here today. Now that you know what the land is going to sell for, you can decide going into this auction if you are willing to pay the price listed on the appraisal. It's that easy."

My cousin listened very quietly and calmly to what I had to say. When I had finished he nodded his head and said, "Okay, Libby." Gosh, no anger?! No outrage?!

No. He seemed to think that what I had just said was reasonable. Which it was. But, gee, then why put everyone through all of those crazy hoops in the first place?!

"Jason," I said with frustration, "if this is okay with you why didn't you just make a similar offer to your aunts and avoid all of this? There is no honor to you this way. You could have acquired the land on your own long ago and avoided all of this mess. Instead, you and your family tried to gyp June and Estelle out of their fair share, even AFTER they were cut out of Grandma's money. It is ridiculous that things have had to come to this to make you pay a fair price to your two old aunts. You ought to be ashamed."

Very softly, he said he wanted to make the offer but... A long silence followed in which Jason would not or could not look me in the eye. He knew that I could complete the rest of that sentence. He would have offered to buy the land outright, but his mother had other ideas and he would never disobey her.

At that point, I felt my anger and frustration at him melt away. Not that I was overcome with warmth and affection, mind you, I just felt such pity toward my cousin. He was a helpless, useless soul who was unlikely ever to have a moment of personal valor or the pride of doing the right thing in the face of adversity. Gosh, he may never even have the satisfaction of making a decision on his own accord. He would spend a lifetime in hand-wringing conflict with himself and the demands he allowed other people to place on him. He would sacrifice his own honor to remain loyal to his mother, regardless of her personal character. Jason would never know the super hero feeling I had just felt a few minutes ago on the courthouse lawn because he would never take a stand for or against anything in which he believed. I didn't hate him for it but I knew I could never respect the person he had become. I actually preferred the superior attitude he had sported in his childhood compared to the hangdog expression he wore that day. It appeared that the boy who was to be king had grown into the court jester. He was too busy trying to please the queen to ever take command of his own kingdom.

I knew then it was time to say goodbye. Not just because the bidding would be starting in a few minutes. It was more than that. I told Jason we would not be seeing each other again after today. I knew our families would be parted for good that time. He said it was too bad it had to be that way but I was probably right. I told him I hoped he ended up with the land, reminding him we wouldn't be driving it up beyond the appraised value, but we had no way of knowing who else might be there to bid and how high they would go. About that time Uncle Lou, Jason's father, was making his way towards us to gather Jason for the auction. I wished my cousin luck and silently passed Uncle Lou and the others coming out of Mr. Baylor's office as I made my way back to the courthouse lawn where Carolyn, Gil and Estelle awaited.

CHAPTER ELEVEN

Carolyn seemed to have regained her composure during my absence and was standing near the steps of the courthouse talking quietly with Gil about the auction that was soon to start. I filled them in on my conversation with Jason and asked how Estelle was getting along. Mom had spent the last hour eating a bowl of ham and beans and talking at some people who were unfortunate enough to have taken a seat beside her at one of the picnic tables. I had gone over there once to check on her and she was busy regaling them with a litany of health problems she had experienced over the past few years. Mom didn't seem to really know or care about what all was taking place around her; she was just enjoying the festival-like atmosphere. I felt a bit guilty leaving her there with those innocent folks but even a super hero can only do so much. Estelle was comfortable and being fed. The fact that she was also being annoying was a secondary concern. I had bigger fish to fry at that moment. Carolyn said she, too, wasn't sure if Mom really knew what all was going on but she seemed to be having a good time and was holding up pretty well.

It was just a few minutes before the auction was scheduled to commence and people began to gather around the main entrance to the courthouse, our kinfolk included. Oretta and her crew were way off to the left side of the steps, with Jason taking a seat on the hood of his truck parked next to the courthouse entrance, putting him a head taller than the crowd around him. I noticed Nedd and his wife, Donna, were not standing with Oretta, but were dispersed among the crowd directly across the lawn from her and to our right. Carolyn, Gil, Mother and I had taken a position directly in front of the steps but a few feet back from the sidewalk on the lawn. It felt like we were flanked by the bad guys and it made me nervous. Carolyn held her tongue but put Mother's arm down to prevent her from waving to our cousin, Laura, one of Oretta's girls. Gil looked calm and cool and seemed ready to play his part.

The auctioneer took his position on the topmost step precisely at 1:00, explained the bidding process, and read the description of the land that was up for sale. The crowd moved in closer to the steps to better hear the proceedings. It appeared even those folks who weren't interested in bidding, but had come to town for the free lunch, figured they might as well stay for the show. Now it would be up to the actual bidders as to who was to get my grandparents' land.

My cousin, Jason, opened the bidding at the outrageously low amount of $50,000. Well, that was okay and to be expected, really. I had no way of knowing if Jason had said anything to his parents about our discussion and perhaps their opening amount had been decided on well in advance. Either way, the low amount worked to our advantage, as it seemed to encourage the crowd, and several people threw out bids. Gil remained silent at that point. He was only there to intervene if the bidding stopped at too low a price. The best case scenario would be for the land to be sold at the appraised value without our involvement.

The bidding continued without us for awhile. I couldn't help but notice Jason looking over to his parents each time before speaking an offer. The price of the land was slowly going up but was still nowhere near the appraised value. The bidders began to drop off one by one until it was just one other man, someone we didn't know, and, of course, Jason. Gil was still very calm and collected but was watching carefully and listening closely. Good thing, too, because I was wound tight as a piano wire and could tell Carolyn was tense, too.

Then it happened. The moment I had been dreading. The stranger bidding against Jason shook his head and dropped out of the bidding at $280,000. Yikes! In my heart I was hoping we could avoid having to get involved in the auction altogether but it was not to be. Gil was going to have to speak a bid. The auctioneer was calling out the going price, "Once..." The selling price at that point was still too low. Way too low. About $200,000 too low. "Twice..." Gil looked at Carolyn and me. Carolyn and I looked at each other. Then we both looked at Gil and nodded and watched as he hollered out a bid of $285,000! We were then officially in the game and I couldn't resist a peek over at Nedd and at Oretta to see their reaction.

What I saw was my second look at genuine shock in one day. I knew instantly Jason had not revealed to his parents the nature of the private conversation we had earlier and they did not expect us to jump into the proceedings and actually bid on the land. Their surprised looks quickly changed to furious faces as they realized they were not going to get that land at any kind of reduced price and we were going to be bidding against them. What they didn't know, because Jason presumably hadn't told them, was that we didn't really want the land. They would naturally be assuming we were trying to buy the land out from under them. Perhaps it was Jason's little way of getting back at his parents; let them sweat it out while he knew darn well what they would be buying the land for in advance. Whatever his reasoning, I knew it was certainly going to make things interesting out there that afternoon. And, with a look and a nod from his father and mother, Jason yelled out his counter bid, upping the price another $5,000.

It went on that way for some time between Jason and Gil. Carolyn's husband was really getting into his role and he took his time placing a bid. Gil would talk to Carolyn and I a little bit and act like we were thinking it over before making a bid another $5,000 over Jason's last offer. Yes, Gil was playing it up and, for Nedd and Oretta, it had the effect of dragging their feet over hot coals. As the selling price peaked over $400,000 the crowd collectively blew out their breath. Those folks had come for a show and they were getting it, brother. I was thinking that little else would be talked about at local cafes for miles around for many days following that auction.

Carolyn was clearly having a good time by that point, too, playing it up with Gil. She had Gil ask the auctioneer a question here or there about the land to keep things interesting. She wanted to know if all of the old tractor parts and household junk that had been dumped at the old home site on the land would be cleaned up. Mostly she wanted to shame and embarrass Oretta with questions like that. I didn't appreciate the way they had been dumping on the land either, but I just wanted that auction to end as soon as possible and wished she would quit monkeying around. It was nerve wracking thinking the whole thing could backfire and we could end up owning some rural Arkansas farm land we most definitely did not want. Just how far would Jason and his parents go? What was their bottom line on bidding for the land? I was strongly hoping it wasn't just short of our own. We had set our final bid figure in advance and Gil was prepared to take it to the line.

The crowd settled back into silence as the bidding slowly continued to inch upward, first by Jason, then with a counteroffer by Gil. My teeth were clenched, waiting for the moment that Jason would shake his head and drop out of the bidding. It could happen, I knew. As the bids grew higher I could see Carolyn's anxiety grow, too. It was as though the three of us, Gil, Carolyn and I, were transfixed by the auctioneer. We couldn't take our eyes off of him, afraid we might miss something at a crucial moment. Then, I knew we were starting to get down to the nitty gritty of that auction when I heard Gil make a bid of $435,000. A silence fell over the crowd. The auctioneer, just as cool and collected as he could be, took a drink of water. Only the tightness in his throat when he tried to swallow that gulp gave away any emotion he may have been feeling from the tension between the bidders at his auction. He calmly set his glass back down and turned his attention to my cousin, Jason, and then to Oretta and Lou.

By that time, I felt like I could lean over onto the grass and lose the cornbread and tea I had eaten for lunch, happy I had at least passed on the ham and beans. Carolyn looked at me with big eyes full of the reality of the situation we were currently facing. Even Gil's face said that he, too, knew we were closing in on the moment we had come for and it just might not work out as we had planned. Would Jason and his parents continue to bid over $435,000? Was that going to be the moment they dropped out? We all looked at Mother who had gotten bored with the auction and was behind us weeding the lawn by pulling out stray dandelions, one of her favorite pastimes at all occasions. She was blissfully ignorant of the importance of the moment.

Lordy, I thought, we may be buying some Arkansas farm land for quite a bit of money in the next few seconds. Almost half million dollars to be exact. Not that we weren't prepared for that moment if it happened. The money would not be a problem. Aunt June had been tickled when we told her about our plan and had agreed to go in on the purchase of the land if the scheme did not work out. We were to get in touch with her by phone after the auction, and I hoped she would remember her promise to assist financially if things backfired on us. Even my brother, Reese, who wanted to stay out of it personally was willing to get involved financially just because the whole idea gave him a good chuckle, too, and he was always open to real estate investments anyway. So, the money was there just in case, but the reality was that none of us wanted that land. We all felt it was time to cut our ties to all Clankton family matters and be done with them once and for all. There was...

"Four hundred eighty-five thousand dollars!"

What?! Who had said that?! Who had jumped the bid up a full $50,000 in one shot?! I had been staring at the ground trying to keep the contents of my stomach at bay and, truth be told, conducting a little private prayer service I hoped would influence the outcome of that day. I looked up and followed the gaze of the entire crowd over to my cousin, Jason, who was looking me straight back in the eye when he calmly, but clearly, repeated his offer, "$485,000."

He had done it! My cousin had finally taken a stand, albeit at the last minute, and put an end to that ridiculous farce. Jason had offered the amount for the land that I told him we were there to insure it sold for that day. A quick glance left, then right, at Oretta and Lou, and at Uncle Nedd, told me everything I needed to know. Unlike the rest of the auction, Jason had evidently made that last offer without seeking his parents' approval first. My aunts and uncles were frozen in awe, open-jawed at the amount of the bid that had just escaped from their front man's lips. The determined look on Jason's face as we stared at each other through the crowd confirmed it. My cousin had made that offer on his own in an attempt to rectify all that had taken place between the family over the business of Grandma's will.

His actions wouldn't change anything within the family at that point, not even between him and me. But it was the right thing to do and it was the first time in my life I had ever felt respect for my cousin. It was very likely that it was the first time he felt respect for himself. I nodded my head to let him know he had done well. I had been wrong. My cousin did get to experience what it felt like to be a super hero. For that moment in his life, Jason was Superman.

As the realization of what had just occurred settled over the crowd, there was a general buzz of conversation and remarks of disbelief. Carolyn turned around to face Gil and me and was grinning ear to ear. Our little group formed a huddle in which we were all giddy with relief and happiness that things had worked out as planned after all. It was a few moments before we realized the auctioneer was awaiting our counter-offer. Gil, with a sense of decorum that I gave him credit for as I wouldn't have been able to utter a word at that point, asked the auctioneer for confirmation of the last bid. The crowd fell back into silence and seemed to be leaning forward in unison as the action on the courthouse steps resumed. The auctioneer repeated the amount loudly and awaited Gil's response. Once again, Gil looked back to Carolyn and me and we both nodded at him. It was time to wrap things up. Gil turned back to the auctioneer and told him that we were not interested in bidding further and the other party may have the land for $485,000. The auctioneer called out the final bid in a loud, clear voice, "Going once... Going twice... SOLD! . .for $485,000!"

With the final words of the auctioneer the crowd went wild, letting out whoops and hollers of surprise at the dollar amount the land had sold for and with relief that the tension of the event was over. Clearly, they had witnessed a show the likes of which that sleepy little town hadn't seen in years! It didn't take long for the parking lot to begin clearing out as folks seemed anxious to be among the first to spread the word to those who had missed that most spectacular ordeal.

Of course, not everyone found amusement in what had taken place. Oretta and her husband, Lou, were already gathered around Jason and nobody in that little group appeared happy. Jason had a look of resolve on his face and I figured he would have to suffer the wrath of his parents. He had been a bad boy and would have to pay a price for his heroism. Literally. A quick glance to my right revealed that Uncle Nedd and his wife weren't looking any too pleased, either. They had remained unobtrusively in the background of the auction that day, apparently content to let the home boy handle the actual bidding. Oretta and Nedd had set up Jason as their front man, making it look as if they weren't involved in that land auction at all, but things hadn't gone quite as planned for them.

As Nedd and Donna approached Oretta's family I could see a quiet fury radiating from Nedd's eyes. He and his wife had clearly come to buy that land at a fraction of its worth, never anticipating anyone bidding against them would pose much of a threat. And it had nearly worked, too. They would have gotten the land for $280,000, about half of what it was worth on the open market, if Gil hadn't jumped in to bid against them. I was guessing, too, they would be hopping mad about having been beaten at their own game, by an enemy they least expected. But really, when all was said and done, they hadn't been cheated. They had simply been kept from cheating anyone else, namely their sisters. Actually, they had some cause to be happy as the final result of that day was that they were the undisputable, rightful owners of Grandma's land. And, let us not forget, they still only had to shell out one half of the selling price, as together Nedd and Oretta owned fifty percent of the land themselves.

I didn't see how anyone could complain about the outcome of the auction, really, but I was sure my angry relatives could have given me a reason or two and I wasn't interested in hanging around to hear them. We had accomplished what we set out to do that day and it was time to move on. Anything exchanged between our rivaling parties was sure to be ugly and I didn't want to mar what had been a rather successful venture up to that point. Therefore, we quickly made our way to the parking lot and by the time Carolyn and I had led Mother over to our vehicle, Gil had untied the pony and loaded him into the trailer. We all settled ourselves in rather quickly and made our move to depart Hattiesville, for the very last time.

As we pulled out of the parking lot Carolyn reached over Gil and gave the horn a couple of short blasts, then leaned out her passenger side window and shouted out to the little group still gathered around Jason, "You all be sure to come on out and visit us sometime!" Good grief, was that necessary?! How my sister and I could be so different I didn't know. I was hoping to make a quiet and dignified exit, letting our success today speak for itself. You know, leave the bad guys pondering their evil ways after good had so clearly triumphed. Carolyn, on the other hand, seemed to feel a need to have the last word and rub it in their faces. I simply sank back into my seat and closed my weary eyes, trying to recall if I'd ever seen any super heroes thumb their noses and heckle the bad guys after they had set them straight.

PART FOUR

THE FAREWELL

CHAPTER TWELVE

Our return trip home was rather uneventful. We had all recited favorite moments from the auction along the way and applauded Gil for playing out his important role so well. Mother was in a pleasant and, of course, talkative mood as she was just happy that we were pleased with the way things had turned out. She still didn't really grasp what had taken place but she was more than willing to celebrate the fact that we seemed to have pulled one over on Oretta and Nedd. Oh, yes, there was a good deal of self-congratulating taking place among our little group, but deep down I wasn't sure if I was entirely comfortable with the way things had turned out. Just like me to be the wet blanket, wishy-washy to the end. I kept my thoughts to myself, though, as I didn't want to dampen everyone's joy at our success. So, as things stood, we all returned to our respective homes waving cheerfully and calling out our final congratulations, feeling happy and contented. Well, almost all of us.

The morning after our return I awoke to my usual routine of making a quick breakfast for myself and heading out for my daily walk. I still had some unsettling feelings gnawing at the back of my brain, and I hoped to be able to shake them off and get on with my day, focusing on the things in my own life that been neglected during the weeks of dealing with Grandma's will and the sale of the land. I needed to come to some kind of resolution with those feelings, and with myself, and find a way to move past all that had happened.

"Oh, come on, give it a rest," I told myself out loud. I needed to get off my high horse and stop analyzing everything. For once, couldn't I just enjoy the moment? After all, we did something that most people only fantasized about doing. How many times had I heard people say they wished they would have done this or they really should have said that? How many times had I said those things myself? Well, Carolyn and Gil and I hadn't just talked about it, we were courageous enough to have actually taken action. It took a lot of effort and persistence to carry out our plan. It was a truly great plan, too, in that it was neither vicious nor damaging. No one got hurt. It was the ultimate act of enforcing justice and fair play in an otherwise rotten situation. It was like something out of a movie or a book. It really was the stuff of legends and super heros. I did feel good about what we had done. I should be happy!

Except I wasn't. In fact, just when I had decided that I should be feeling fantastic... I started to cry. I stopped walking and simply let the tears flow for a few moments, using the tail of my t-shirt to wipe my runny nose and watery eyes. Oh, boy, I am a piece of work, I thought to myself. If Carolyn could see me now, she would walk away in disgust, barely resisting the temptation to slap me across my wimpy, wet face. Well, I couldn't help it. Besides, what I was feeling right then did not really involve Carolyn anyway. It was personal. I was crying for a reason. I was crying, of course, because I had just experienced a terrible loss.

Oh, yes, it was true, my Grandmother had passed away and I had been sad about her death. But that had taken place almost a year ago and she had lived to the ripe old age of ninety-three. That day after the auction I was mourning the loss of other family members. Lots of them. Two uncles, two aunts, eight cousins and, yes, even three crazy little dogs in diapers. I had not lost them to death, but to greed and weakness of character. Somehow, losing them all at once and under those circumstances seemed particularly tragic and untimely.

As I stood in the middle of the deserted trail I had walked down, I gave myself permission to grieve their loss. I cried until I could cry no more. I cried because all of those family members were out of my life forever. I cried because of the type of people I had discovered they really were and the pain it caused me. I cried because my aunt and uncle had willingly sacrificed their relationship with me and my sister and my mother over the prospect of gaining a few dollars.

I cried, too, that day because I had a terrible feeling that out of the entire Clankton family, my mother and sister included, I would be the only one doing any crying. I doubted anyone else would recognize, let alone mourn, the loss we had all experienced over the last several weeks. Oh, Oretta and Nedd may focus on the loss of the money they will have to shell out for payment on the land, but not on Estelle's, or Carolyn's or my absence in their lives. Carolyn and Mother themselves were unlikely to feel any loss on their part either, instead focusing on the successful sale of the land at the auction and their victory over the contemptuous Oretta and Nedd. Mom would not remember much more than that, while Carolyn would never forget, or forgive.

Now, I knew that many folks would simply have said good riddance to them all and wonder why I was carrying on so over the elimination of a bunch of no good relatives from my life. Like cousin Jason, for example, with his cowardly demeanor and inability to take control of his own life. Or Uncle Nedd, who had been a user and a loser from day one. And especially like Aunt Oretta, with her insecure behavior and critical tongue, irritating accent, and deceitful manipulation of Grandma's will. Heck, Oretta and I didn't like each other anyway, right?

Right. All of those things were true. What was bothering me was the very fact that they had always been true. I had spent time with those people on and off for almost forty years and they had always been the same selfish, hostile, funny, hateful, kind, crazy characters that I knew and, yes, even loved. The difference was that during all of those years I had accepted them for who and what they were. But I was no longer willing to do that. I was choosing to give them up in the same way they had chosen to forfeit my presence in their lives. I had placed Oretta's and Nedd's greed for cold, hard cash above our personal relationship, just as they had; them by choosing to keep Grandma's money and attempting to profit from the sale of the land by cheating their siblings, and I by disassociating from the kind of people who would do either of those things. I didn't regret my decision, but having been forced into making it was painful.

Having come to some kind of an understanding with myself, I was starting to feel a bit better. I wiped away a final tear and took a long, deep breath. For me, only then was it all truly over. I did feel good about what Carolyn, Gil and I had accomplished. I also felt sad about what had been sacrificed throughout the ordeal. Most importantly, the whole event had made me think a great deal about myself and the relationships I have with my own mother and siblings.

As I began to walk slowly toward home, I thought of how ugly things could get where money was involved, even among the closest of friends and family. Maybe especially so then. Suddenly, it dawned on me that although the entire process of dealing with Grandma's will was put to rest where I was concerned, the fate of Oretta and Nedd's alliance was far from resolved. I shook my head and grimaced at the thought of what lay ahead for those two scallywags. Some people never learned. Oh, they would operate for awhile under the delusion of being faithful business partners, but it wouldn't last. It's just not in their Clankton blood. That little honeymoon will be over before too long and those two will be going at that piece of land like dogs over a bone. For one thing, Oretta laid claim to that land long ago, and I doubt that she had any real intentions of sharing its profits with Nedd. After all, her family had farmed that land for years while Nedd turned up his nose at offers of the land from his parents because farming was too lowly for the likes of him. It will be of no surprise to anyone when those old claims and entitlements, insults and accusations spill forth. It was just a matter of time. Oh, yes, a Clankton feud would rise in the south again one day. But it would be a battle fought without me.

I know, now, that I will not fight my own brother and sister over the will our mother, Estelle, leaves behind, regardless of what it might say. If our mother leaves everything to me, I will equally divide everything with Carolyn and Reese. Instantly. If Mother excludes me out of her will altogether I will accept that, too, and allow Reese and Carolyn to do what they feel is just, without repercussion. After all, my relationship with Mother has never been about money. I have received little assistance, financial or otherwise, from her in the course of my life. The basis of my relationship with my unique mother is so much more complex and compelling than cash. If her money has played no part in my relationship with her while she is living, why on earth would it be the most important thing about her death?

With that frame of mind, I am willing to accept whatever is to happen in my own family, as I now believe where there's a will, there is also a way to preserve what is most important in life. I intend to find it.

Lucinda Perry holds a Master's Degree in Educational Psychology and is a former school counselor. She currently resides on a cattle ranch in eastern Colorado with her husband, Dean. Where There's A Will *is her first novel.*

Printed in the United States
16701LVS00002B/196-294

9 781592 990535